Tourist

SCEPTRE

Tourist

MATT THORNE

SCEPTRE

First published in 1998 by Hodder and Stoughton
A division of Hodder Headline PLC
A Sceptre Book

10 9 8 7 6 5 4 3 2 1

A CIP catalogue record for this book is available from the British Library

ISBN 0 340 70864 6

Typeset by Palimpsest Book Production Limited,
Polmont, Stirlingshire
Printed and bound in Great Britain by
Mackays of Chatham PLC, Chatham, Kent

Hodder and Stoughton
A division of Hodder Headline PLC
338 Euston Road
London NW1 3BH

For Zoë

Acknowledgements

Rachel Brittain, Bronze Age Fox, A.S. Byatt, Douglas Dunn, Tibor Fischer, Greg, Barbara and Beth Gardner, Nick Guyatt, John Harvey, Chris King, Carl MacDougall, Steve McCoy, Steve Merchant, Claire Preston, Jonathan Pritchard, Neil Taylor, Louise, Dave and Kaye Thorne, and Simon Trewin

Friday

It takes five steps to get into the light. With every step I expect to be knocked flat. Not being attacked seems like not paying my phonebill: sooner or later someone's bound to catch up with me.

What Every Woman Wants fulfilled its pledge by illuminating my path through Dolphin Square. Alongside me, evergreen trees arose from fish-papered flowerbeds. No deodorant could cope with a summer shift, and the underarms of my bowling shirt had darkened from scarlet to vermilion. I almost shat myself when someone took my arm.

It was Paul.

'How much do you charge?' he asked, smiling.

I looked at him, felt my anger die down, then decided to play along: 'A bag of chips, maybe. Depends on the man.'

'I can stretch to that. Come on, love, let's get you fed.'

We walked down past Coffins Coffee Shop and the Seaside Restaurant. The streets had been dry for a week and it was hard to ignore the sour-smelling drains. The closed arcades glowed purple and orange, like secret laboratories.

Few people were out. Twelve until one is a quiet hour, a time for refuelling.

'Do you know anything about business, love?'

'Enough to earn a living.'

'No, not that sort of work. I'm not knocking it, the oldest trade and all that. But I'm talking about business.'

'I can do a good secretary,' I told him. 'Take dictation, type fifty words a minute.'

'I was thinking more along the lines of a personal assistant,' he said. 'Someone to take care of my individual needs.'

We joined the queue from The Cod Plaice. Inside, a man dared his girlfriend to touch the top of the oven. The woman smiled and pressed her fingers onto the hot metal, holding them there without showing any sign of pain.

I took Paul's arm. 'So what line are you in?'

'Entertainment.'

I laughed.

'What's funny?' he asked.

'Every man I meet says he's in entertainment. Seems like a lot of hot air to me.'

My voice faltered. Paul glared at me. I'd struck a wrong note, made his game seem stupid. Usually he'd talk over a gap like this, but tonight he let the pause play out, disappointment setting in behind his brown eyes. He'd never met me from the bowling alley before. I wondered if he thought he'd made a mistake.

It was Paul's turn to order. Smiling at the woman serving, he said: 'How would you like to see your name up in lights?'

Paul's teeth flashed as he bit a hole in his ketchup sachet. He has poor teeth, the crooked canines the key to everything that is wrong with his face. He rolled the sachet like a toothpaste tube to drain every drop. He ate his chips in handfuls, and his chin and shirt were soon speckled with stray sauce.

'You can always tell the quality of a girl,' he told me, 'by the way she eats her chips.'

'And what quality am I?' I asked, pleased to be given a second chance.

'Oh, you're the best. A category I call superior. It's always great to watch a superior girl eat chips.'

'Why?'

'Because it gives you an idea of what's to come.'

'Excuse me?'

He wiped his lips with the back of his hand. 'A superior girl is the perfect midpoint between a snob and a slag. No one wants to watch a slag eat chips because she just stuffs them in her gob with no refinement at all. And watching a snob eat chips is like watching someone being tortured. You feel like you've given her a cone of rusty nails. Now, at first, a superior girl looks like she isn't going to enjoy her chips. Her hands go all birdlike, she bends and flutters them so she doesn't get any grease or ketchup on her fingers but, and this is the important part, she likes chips. In fact, she loves chips. It's just that she understands it's all got to be done with a degree of art.'

He smiled. Behind Paul stood the Grand Pier, once the highlight of any Weston trip. Now I rarely thought about it. I tried, that second, to remember visiting it as a child, but all I could recall was the discomfort of a nylon swimsuit, and one sad Sunday afternoon spent dropping coins through the wooden slats for my sister to catch before they hit the beach below. But I didn't want to think about this with Paul beside me. So I asked him: 'Where next?'

'Do you do home visits?'

Paul was always trying to shock me, but this was the first time he'd succeeded. Before now he'd always come over to

Sylvia's, or parked his car behind the big Tesco. I'd never been to his house, and had assumed my boss would like to stay with his dutiful employee tonight.

'Anyway, you're wrong,' I told him. 'The reason why my hands go all fluttery is because of the rings on my fingers. They change the way I eat.'

'Don't spoil the illusion, love.'

'I know, I know,' he said, 'I bought it in my dry period. I'd just moved down and couldn't afford anything special. But don't write it off until you've been inside. I've got everything.'

As he fiddled with his keys, I was touched by his nervousness. From behind, I could see the bald spot and the paste beads of gel not properly combed in, the creased jacket and the splitting leather at the back of each heel. I always felt anxious when Paul got talkative, pleased he was confiding in me but worried in case it was a prelude to a crash.

'Treats?' he suggested.

'What sort?'

'Pink Champagne.'

'No thanks,' I told him, 'not tonight.'

I looked away while he went through his routine. Then he said: 'What I want to do, what I've always wanted to do, is to get in and make the next development myself. As far as I can see, now that they've got the attention of the families and the teenagers, the only market left is the adults. Particularly men. Take tonight. We walked through Weston on a Saturday night and there were men on every street with nothing to do. If you can't find a slag, you either get into a fight or you go home to bed. I want to offer an alternative.

'When I was in London, I stuck to the markets I knew, but I had connections in every industry. And everyone knew the real money was in strip clubs. Now I'm not suggesting that. But what about something more refined? Glamorous, but refined. A gentleman's club. Well, a cabaret club, really, like you get abroad. But with a twist.'

He swallowed. 'As I understand it, entertainment is about escape. But in Weston, the only people who really get to escape are the kids. What if I could recreate that magic for everyone? Think of it this way. Where's the one place that still holds mystery? The one place we know nothing about?'

'Heaven?'

'Space.'

I looked at him. He grinned and said: 'I want people to believe they're guests in a giant spaceship, noblemen of the future being entertained on their way to a distant planet. Like a luxury cruise, only through space instead of the ocean. We'll have pianos, cocktails, imaginary spacescapes behind imaginary windows. We'll get the most beautiful girls in Weston to be hatcheck and matchstick girls. Only we'll give them one strange feature to make them look alien. Then the show will be like an old-time show, with comedians, singers, strippers, all that. And it will last all night. Then, at dawn, the last act will be us.

'We'll be the hosts, but more importantly, we'll be ambassadors. You'll have the most incredible dress. We'll get it made specially, I know someone in the business. And we'll seem like gods to everyone else. The captain and his mistress. The most glamorous, exciting couple in the whole universe.'

So what do you think of Paul's pitch? I have to confess I started dreaming when I heard his words. I went for a shower so he couldn't see my pleasure and hold it against me when the scheme fell through. I felt angry at myself for getting excited by my lover's daft plan, but even as I thought this I was pushing back my fringe and posing. This was how he drew me in the first time. His deceptive ad: *recruitment for a job in the entertainment industry*. Then in the interview, he told me he was pleased I was from London because that meant I knew about glamour. After compliments like that, I was happy to promise Paul my loyalty.

It was a woman's bathroom. Paul's toiletries were confined to the cabinet, while Iona's cosmetics curled across every available surface. Facial scrub, nail varnish, primrose oil, perfume. I considered squirting her scent across my skin, just to see if Paul'd notice. But I knew that if I did and Paul told me I smelt nice, it'd depress me. So I unpopped my bowling top and pulled it over my head. My red and brown uniform looked like an ugly stain across the pink carpet. I climbed behind the glass screen and turned the dial to power shower, thinking it was the setting Paul's wife was least likely to use, then closed my eyes to take off in the spaceship again.

I used to feel proud of my body. The first time I had sex with Paul, I couldn't believe my generosity, and took his tears as an acknowledgement of my charity. Since then, I've slowly lost faith in the value of my thin limbs and neat waist, and my muscles hold on to Paul when he is inside me instead of nonchalantly tolerating the intrusion.

I chose Paul because I knew too much about the bodies of younger men. When I was a kid a schoolfriend told me that the average penis got longer with every subsequent generation. I still don't know if this is fact or myth, but in my experience, the younger the man, the less there is to write home about. And on the few occasions I've found a worthwhile weight swinging between tender thighs, it's always seemed incongruous, as if they've stolen the weapon from their fathers and feel scared of marking it.

With Paul, I wanted a distance to make it a challenge, to ignore sentiment and concentrate on physical reactions. But the fine hairs on his torso and legs are like the pencil shadings that give a picture depth, and once I'd noticed them his body became as individual as any other boyfriend I'd had. I knew the exact number of moles on his back, the depth of his belly button. And although he wasn't the only man I slept with, whenever I thought about sex I pictured Paul, and whenever I fantasised about someone new I always gave them Paul's arms and chest.

I've never understood why people name their cars but not their furniture. Every time we made love in Paul's car, I felt we were injecting life into a passionless metal box, the stilled machine oblivious to our coupling. But beds are conspiratorial, pleased to be in on the action but burdened by the betrayals they're forced to witness. Slipping between Paul's sheets that night, I felt a strange affection for the springs of his mattress, sensing their reluctance with every strained bounce.

When our breathing had returned to normal, I felt Paul's hand on my shoulder.

'Don't go to sleep yet,' he told me.

'Sorry Paul, I'm really tired. Don't forget I had a day in the office before my bowling shift.'

'You should have taken some speed with me.'

'I'm too tired for it to have any effect. But if you want to talk I'll try to stay awake.'

'No, don't bother. You'll never manage it. If I so much as pause, you'll drop off.'

'But you won't pause.'

He laughed. 'That's true.'

'Perhaps you could pretend I was awake. If you say anything important I'm sure it'll filter through.'

'No, it's okay. I'll shut up. You go to sleep.'

'Are you sure?'

'Yes. You have my permission.'

I felt hot and itchy, so I kicked back the sheets and hugged his wife's pillow to my face. I could feel Paul fidgeting but his pokes couldn't keep me awake. It was a deep sleep, and the only dream I could remember the next morning began with a television presenter standing on purple sand in front of an orange sea, explaining how 'a new mystery had excited the usually placid inhabitants of Weston Super Mare in a totally unprecedented manner'.

'If you've seen the adverts for The Pleasure Palace,' he told the camera, 'then you'll already know that this is no ordinary nightclub. Tonight we'll be talking to the owner, self-made entertainment baron, Paul March, and taking a look at a cabaret show so modern it takes place in the future.'

I knew I was dreaming, but tonight that knowledge was comforting rather than disappointing. I wanted to see how Paul'd changed, but the interview was skipped and the dream continued with the end of the show. I stood in front of a crowd of unfamiliar faces, wearing a black evening dress that was too long for me, making it look as if my legs had melted into the floor. I was also wearing a heavy brown wig and unflattering jewellery. Two tentacles grew out from either side of my neck. I waited in the spotlight alone, a microphone in front of me. The audience applauded, the band struck up, and I opened my mouth to sing.

Monday

The new recruits arrived today.

All last night Paul kept saying, 'the new recruits, the new recruits', and every time he said it we laughed and had another drink. Paul'd been generous to me all weekend, remaining calm even when I went to see Henry on Sunday. I kept expecting to be told to leave, but the command didn't come. Eventually I asked if Iona had gone for good. 'No,' he told me, 'just the weekend, so enjoy it while it lasts.'

Every summer Paul employs one man and one woman. He says he picks students because they'll do anything he tells them, but that's not the reason. Students take him seriously, and he thinks if enough people treat him like a boss, he'll finally become one.

One man, one woman. I pick the man, he picks the woman. He thinks this gives the operation a family feel. This year's chosen two: Neil Renard and Mary Excell. I'd deliberately gone for a conservative man this time, knowing Paul expected me to goad him with someone outrageous. Going on Paul's past form, Mary'd either be stylish and quiet or soon to be successful, someone he wanted a piece of early on.

I stood on the platform holding a clipboard, a visual clue for the recruits. I scanned the blondes leaving the 9.25. Then Mary approached me.

'Are you Sarah?'

I stared at her. 'Yes.'

'I'm Mary.'

She offered her hand. I shook it.

'Right,' I said, trying not to look flustered.

She was wearing a long silver raincoat and PVC trainers, her black hair cut in a feathered style I was surprised had become fashionable again.

'So,' she said, 'are we going to the office?'

'In a little while. We have to pick up Neil first.'

I took her across to the Off the Rails café. The people inside glared at me, angry to be reminded of daylight. As I held the door open for Mary, they gathered together and rose up, trying to generate their own darkness. Everyone looked as if they were already at the end of a heavy evening, and I wondered if the waitress had deliberately smeared her make-up to make them feel more comfortable. I asked Mary what she wanted to drink, meaning tea or coffee. She hesitated, then asked for a Kronenbourg.

I brought her the drink and a packet of nuts.

'Good omen,' she said.

'What?'

'The jukebox.'

I stared at her.

'The Stones,' she said. '"Spider and the Fly".'

I poured the milk into my coffee. Mary pointed at a poster behind me. 'Shame we're going to miss him.'

I turned round. It was a photo of a man wearing a zebra-patterned jacket and silver glasses. His long blond hair receded way past his forehead and he strained over a banjo, whole face scrunched into a leering grin. *Old Bob Crud,* it said in green letters. *He says he's shit. We say he's shit. Don't say we didn't warn you.*

'So what else is there to do in this town?'

'There's the Buzz,' I told her, 'and The Imperial, and the Europa, and The Princess, and a weird Goth place. But if you're serious about clubbing there's loads of weekenders.'

Mary nodded and sipped her pint. I waited for her next question but she kept quiet, staring at the fruit machine in the corner. She had a low forehead and stubborn eyes, and after five minutes in her company, I still had no idea what Paul'd seen in her. I looked at my watch and urged the next train to arrive.

Neil climbed down onto the platform. He looked younger than he had in the interview, and I found it hard to recall why I thought Paul would like him. His face glowed with the tailend of teenage skin, the cigarette ember colour strangely attractive. His shoulders were pinched together by a huge backpack that made him stagger for the first few steps. I rescued him and introduced him to Mary.

March Entertainments is located above a solarium. Day one's always serious. Paul's a good speaker, and his rhetoric hides the flimsiness of our operation. He has the props too, writing on whiteboards with Xylene-free pens. He wanted to give the recruits mobile phones, but I talked him down to pagers. BT Lyrics. At first he suggested we should all have one, to increase the feeling of intimacy between us. But I told him I hated the idea of being constantly badgered and he said I didn't have to wear one.

I sat alongside Paul as he lectured, marvelling at the clever way he broke down the business for them. His best trick is convincing the recruits that their mundane tasks (selling ad space, neon displays, laminated plastic menus) are the most important part of March Entertainments. I'm always surprised at how easily they accept this notion, until I remind myself how long I remained in ignorance of Paul's shadier dealings.

I was still trying to get the measure of Mary. According to my clipboard, she comes from Kensington, so maybe her background isn't that different from mine. A second-year Textiles student at Nottingham Uni. That'd explain the strange dress.

'Lunchtime,' finished Paul, flicking off the OHP. 'When you get back, we'll go on a field trip.'

Neil looked at Mary. She ignored him, taking her coat from the chair. It was too hot for two layers, let alone a plastic mac. I followed Paul into the office.

'So what d'you think?' he said.

'You want the truth?'

'Of course.'

'I don't know what the fuck you were thinking.'

He laughed. 'Are you jealous?'

'What?'

'Perhaps you think my taste has changed.'

'I was thinking about business. When you interviewed me you said glamour was an important part of the job. She looks like an astronaut.'

'What about Neil?' he asked. 'I thought you said he was like me.'

'He was, in the interview. I don't know why he's gone quiet.'

'Will we lose him?'

'Hard to tell. But we have the back-up.'

'I'd like to hang on to Neil if we can. So make an effort. Draw him out.' He picked up the phone. 'Now, what d'you want for lunch?'

'First thing you have to understand,' Paul began, leading us towards the Sea Front, 'this ain't telesales. You can't do promotions from behind a desk. You have to get a feel for the place. Selling displays is easy enough but you've got to sucker them into the whole package. Most people in Weston are suspicious and stupid. That gives you an advantage.'

He stopped outside the Beachsands Hotel. A man in a black satin vest stared at us through his Sierra's dirty windscreen, licking ice cream from his ginger moustache.

'Most companies will load you down with regulations, inhibit your creativity with some stupid image you're supposed to project. March Entertainments isn't like that. I've employed you. Now I'm prepared to trust you. The one instruction I will give is never be scared to act on your instincts. Most promotions people tell you to talk to the owners, concentrate your attack on the people with money. Fair enough. But that's not the only way to do business. You're young, so mix with the temporary staff. Make friends with the sons and daughters of the families who run the hotels. The trick is to get invited to talk about your work. Be secretive. Surprise me.'

I sat in Paul's office waiting for him to finish up for the day. He made one final phonecall that turned into three final phonecalls, then we left together. As we drove past Emmanuel Church, I noticed Neil staggering along with his huge bag. Paul slowed the car and told him to get in.

'Where to?' Paul asked.

'I don't really have a room yet,' he said, 'so take me to a cheap B and B.'

'Is it Economics you're studying at university?'

'That's right.'

'And what do you want to do eventually?'

'Work in the City. And drive a car like this.'

Paul smiled. 'Would you be offended if I told you a cautionary story? About working in the City and driving nice cars?'

He turned in his seat. Neil shook his head.

'I've never actually worked in the City,' Paul began, 'but I've invested heavily. Before that, I worked as a tally man. Do you know what that is?'

'Is it like a Christmas Club?' Neil asked.

'Sort of. I began by lending people money, but that seemed too shady and I worried I might run into some real loan sharks who might take exception to my dabbling. So I started buying items for people. That way I could get the discounts through paying cash while they scrimped to pay me the original price plus interest. Soon I had enough to buy in bulk from warehouses. I had a whole range of stuff and I'd go round selling it out of a suitcase.'

I looked at Paul, surprised he was telling this story again. He looked back to the rear-view.

'I spent five years going door-to-door. I should've got out of it sooner, but I got used to the life. It was fun seeing different people every day. More people stayed at home then, and every time you went into a new house you'd get caught up in a little story.

'But anyone who's out to make money soon runs into other entrepreneurs, and I got involved with this group of builders, a kind of secret society made up of friends of friends. They had all this property they were developing and they needed investors. I started with a small stake, but every time I made any money I put it all back in.

'Most of the investors were older than me, and more prepared to wait for a return on their money. I didn't have time to sit around, and wanted to go it alone. If I'd stuck with those builders, I'd have a fleet of nice cars instead of just one. When the property slump came, my money was spread everywhere and I got washed out. There was no one to protect me. It's taken me a long time to recover from that.'

Neil was silent. After a moment, Paul asked, 'So tell me something. What's the economic viability of you being able to stay in a Bed and Breakfast?'

'Good,' he said. 'Well, maybe not the breakfast.'

Paul laughed and looked at me. 'What about La Wrench? Surely she has room for the boy?'

I swallowed. 'There's always an open door at Sylvia's.'

'Right,' he said, 'then I'll drop you off together.'

Reception was empty. Sylvia's daughter was vacuuming the dining room, pulling up the flex so she could get to the skirting board. A smear of mint toothpaste partially covered the love bite on her neck. I watched her legs move back and forth, then asked: 'Where's your mum?'

'It's Bingo night. She'll be back around ten.'

I didn't want Neil to see my room but I couldn't leave him in the lounge. Cursing Paul, I took Neil up to Room Seven, and asked him to wait outside while I picked up my clothes, rearranged the sheets and threw a blanket over my desk.

'Come in.'

Neil looked around my room. I felt a quiver of embarrassment every time his eyes rested on anything. It was silly, but I felt intimidated by his presence, convinced he could see through the mattress to the dirty clothes I'd kicked beneath it. 'Who are those women on your wall?' he asked. 'Your sisters?'

'No,' I laughed, 'they're actresses.'

'Who's the one on the left?'

'Teri Garr.'

'She looks like you.'

'I hope I don't look so depressed.'

'She doesn't look depressed. She's smiling.'

I looked at the photograph. As stupid as it sounds, I've lived with that picture on my wall for three years and never noticed Teri smiling. I don't think I even looked at her mouth. I looked at her eyes, the slump in her shoulders, and all I saw was a weary resignation that I completely understood.

Neil turned to me.

'Don't worry,' he said, 'I won't get a room here.'

I stared at him, amazed he'd read my worries so perceptively. His respectful tone made me feel petty.

'It's not you,' I told him. 'I don't know what it is.'

He laughed. 'You and Paul, are you involved?'

I didn't say anything. He smiled.

'I thought so.'

5

Tuesday

Mary entered Paul's office. Her sleeveless top was too tight for her, the blue logo fighting for space between her breasts. Paul looked up.

'Problem?'

'No.' She looked at me. 'Sarah, do you still want to go for lunch?'

'Just let me finish this.'

Mary squeezed her gum into the ashtray. She left the office in three curved strides, as if her legs were a pair of compasses. Paul studied my face.

'I thought you didn't like her.'

'That was yesterday.'

'I see,' he said. 'Is there anywhere else that might buy ad space?'

'We could try along the pier. Perhaps send Mary.'

'And get her to flog signs at the same time?'

'Good idea.'

Mary pressed her face against the window of Paul's door. He laughed. 'Go on then, we can finish this later.'

'Are you desperate to eat? Only I thought we could stroll down to the pier instead.'

She shrugged and we started walking. Saturday night's storm had done little to relieve the swampy atmosphere. The June sun is a puritan, using his brilliance to expose the weakness of those beneath him. Today the damp had settled on the backs of my thighs, forcing me to keep picking at my dress.

The T-shirts had started. Only two today. A fat man confessing 'Sticks and Stones will Break my Bones, but Whips and Chains Excite me' and an eleven-year-old with 'Look, Don't Touch' across her tiny buds. Last summer, I saw so many I almost bought one myself, unable to decide between 'Enjoy Cock' and 'Have a Kwik-Krap'.

I made Mary sit in the yellow plastic train that takes tourists to the front of the Grand Pier. It was no distance to walk, but I wanted her to have the full Weston experience. Most parts of the town have a specific scent, but at the front of the pier every smell combines, the dominant aroma dependent on where you direct your nose. Turn north and you'll get the baby's burp of candy floss, lasting 180° before your nostrils are assaulted by the south's sea sewage. To the east lies donkey shit, while the best the west can offer is a meaty odour pumped out through the extractor fans of the Sea Front restaurants.

Mary seemed nervous so I tried to calm her down with the arm pat my mother uses to befriend strangers. Only I must have done it wrong because now she looked terrified.

'So what d'you think of Weston?'

She looked at me as if I'd invented the place. 'I don't know,' she said, 'I haven't settled in yet.'

The small boy next to Mary kept glancing at her breasts, gripping himself through his faded blue shorts. Mary ignored him, but I couldn't help envying the infant's freedom. I considered staring back at him and responding in kind, but didn't want to further disturb my guest.

'Want a rolly?' she asked.

I shook my head. Mary took a pouch of Drum tobacco from her PVC handbag. Her purple varnish drew attention to her Frankenstein fingernails, a feature I hadn't noticed before. Watching her fiddle with that ratty thing made me crave a real cigarette, but I've gone twenty-seven days without one and didn't feel ready to give in yet.

The train stopped and I stepped down onto the pier. A man with a tray of sunglasses approached us, reflecting light into our eyes.

'Shades, ladies? Two pound the Lennons, three quid the Ednas.'

'Maybe later,' said Mary. The man nodded, as if this was a firm arrangement. He turned to me. I shrugged, then walked past him.

The Grand Pier is the friendliest of Weston's arcades. Few machines here have cash payouts, instead dispensing orange tickets that can be exchanged for prizes at the Gift Booth. As these rewards are heart-hugging gorillas, crying china children and evil marionettes, the place holds little attraction for anyone other than grannies and young families.

I looked at Mary. I knew she wouldn't give anything away until I did. So I said: 'Neil's nice, isn't he?'

'Not really my type.'

'What's your type?'

She smiled. 'I like people who are a little bit strange.'

'Strange how?'

'Men I'm not supposed to like. I went to public school and spent six years sucking off Sebastians. Now I choose. It could be anyone. Plasterers, painters and decorators, road sweepers.'

'Sounds like we have something in common.'

'Paul's not strange.'

'I'm not talking about Paul.'

'Who then?'

'Paul's not the only man I see. I have another lover who's weird enough.'

'Weird how?'

'He's a rich old man.' I made my way through the banks of machines, knowing Mary'd follow. 'When I first told Paul I was seeing someone else he spent weeks getting paranoid about this young guy he wouldn't be able to keep up with. I thought he'd be relieved when he found out about Henry.'

'But he wasn't?'

'No.'

I stopped in front of Tin Cat Alley, watching the black and white cat as he peeked at us from the safety of his metal dustbin. I put in fifty pence, handed Mary some balls and pressed the start button.

'Ready?'

Pank. Pank. Pank.

'He said I betrayed him. He said I chose Henry deliberately to piss him off. Part of the reason Paul came to Weston was because Henry said he'd give him the money to start up a new operation, and he hates the idea of me sleeping with him. Personally, I think it pulls everything nicely together, like tying a double knot in a shoelace.'

Pank. Pank. Pank.

Mary reached down for more balls. 'I'm surprised he doesn't sack you.'

'Most men would. Most men I wouldn't dream of challenging like that. But Paul's different.'

'How?'

'He fucked up. He doesn't want to be in Weston. He doesn't really want to work for his money. The only way he survives is by treating the whole thing as some kind of macho competition. If I present him with a few challenges, he'll think he's proving himself by rising to them.'

Pank.

'That sounds a bit simplistic.'

'Maybe, but it's worked so far.'

The cat disappeared into his can for the final time. Two tickets emerged from the slot. I pocketed them.

'How's your basketball?'

'Never played. I was on the netball team at school.'

'Same difference.'

We walked across to the basketball machine. I fed it fifty pence and it played 'The Star-Spangled Banner'. I pressed start and the gate rose, letting several balls roll towards us. We took it in turns, Mary shooting from the bottom, me from the top. Neither of us was particularly accurate, but we managed to gain one ticket.

'Another game?'

'Okay, but let me pay.'

We swapped positions and I stared at Mary's arms as she fired balls towards the hoop. Her biceps were tighter than mine, but I took comfort from the fact that the muscles were part of a rather obvious bodyshape, her tight legs, arms and breasts unable to hide the large bones beneath her flesh. When the last ball clanked down behind the closed gate, I asked: 'So why are you here?'

She stared at me.

'No one comes to Weston without a story,' I told her. 'There's no life left in mine, but yours must be new.'

'I like the sea.'

I laughed. 'Yeah, I've used that one. The pollution was getting to you and you were going to spend your summer in Brighton, but *everyone* goes to Brighton, so you thought you'd try somewhere a little less obvious.'

She didn't answer.

'Ever seen the holiday guide for Weston Super Mare? One

super smile after another, it says on the cover. Maybe that's what brought you here.'

She sniffed. 'It's only a summer job. It's impossible to get vacation work in London.'

'What about abroad?'

'I can't afford to get there. Besides, I want a job that isn't taxing.'

We stopped outside the Gift Booth. It looked like a contestant's sweep from *The Generation Game,* each item tagged with its value and laid out on red velour.

'We can't get much, I'm afraid.'

She looked over my shoulder. 'Is that a Queen of Hearts machine?'

'I don't know.'

'It is. I'll get us some tickets.'

She walked over to this machine, her stiff-legged arcs relaxing into a loose swagger. The game was simple. Five cards, face up, one Queen, four Kings. The cards go down. You find the lady. After sixty tickets, I asked Mary if she had this game at home.

She laughed. 'I'm just good at observing things, that's all. When I was little my mother made me do memory exercises. Spot the difference sort of stuff. So now I have a knack for it.'

Mary looped the tickets round her fist and returned to the Gift Booth.

'See anything you like?' I asked.

'I don't know,' she said, looking into the cabinet.

'The more tickets you have, the more things you don't want.'

'I think I'll get some sunglasses. Fend off that salesman outside.'

'Which ones? Porky Pig? Pepe le Pew?'

'Minnie Mouse, I think. The blue ones.'

She told the attendant and he unclipped a pair from the

cardboard display. Mary slipped them on and we walked back into the sun. I looked at my watch.

'Maybe we do have time for lunch after all.'

Paul capped and uncapped a whiteboard marker, waiting for me to explain. He always looks uneasy during office hours, rarely relaxing before the afterwork drink.

'Where d'you go?' he asked

'Just the sandwich shop.'

'So you and Mary are friends now?'

'Is that okay?'

'Of course.' He swallowed. 'Sarah, you're not doing the Dolphin on Wednesday, are you?'

'No. Why?'

'I thought we might have another night together.'

'At your house?'

'If you like.'

'Okay.'

'Thanks.'

He nodded and stood up. He reached across and patted me on the shoulder, then left the office. I stared into the fractal patterns emerging on my lover's computer screen, praying he wasn't about to split from his wife.

5

Thursday

I managed one year of university. Every night I'd test myself, seeing if I could get through a whole evening alone. At first the challenge was too daunting and I'd cheat, getting my friends to come round and interrupt me. I'd envisaged this as a temporary caution, but after a few weeks my hospitality was taken for granted, leaving few undergraduates who didn't plan their evenings around a trip to my room.

Their stories were so tragic I felt scared to go out, worried some horsy girl would be so distraught by my absence that she'd throw herself from the roof of the cafeteria. I had to postpone my nightly bath to twelve or later, depending on how long it took my last caller to finish their complaints. Every evening I cooked my pasta with some pompous preppy prowling round the kitchen, peeking into my pans while he told me why his girlfriend ought to feel lucky, and always ate it with two bulimics watching from my bed.

My only consolation for standing ready with green china mugs of fruit-flavoured tea was knowing how much my confidants valued me. I looked forward to the student magazine, imagining a eulogy from some suicide case I'd saved without noticing. I imagined the titles about to be bestowed on me: most sympathetic listener, the year's secret crush.

The magazine came out and I wasn't in it. Worse still, every other undergraduate appeared to have already experienced six relationships, four scandals and at least one near-death experience. Few stories tallied with the secrets I'd been told, and my knowledge of my fellow students' inner lives proved much less comprehensive than I imagined. I went home and spent the vacation brooding over my betrayal, reading about the parties I'd missed and feeling the most unpopular I'd felt since childhood.

I tried to remember this time last night, wanting to convince Paul I understood his frustration. When I agreed to come to his house again, I knew at some point he'd want to talk, and had already decided acting sympathetically would be the quickest way to get us back to normal.

My skill as a mistress is fired by aptitude rather than appetite. I don't want to become the next Mrs March, and the wobbles in Paul's relationship worry rather than excite me. Nor do I enjoy being inside another woman's house, and have never been the type to get a thrill from deceit. I'm simply blessed with a talent that doesn't match my character, like a nun with a knack for the butterfly flick.

After dinner, Paul searched for his Pink Champagne. I'd considered stealing it, knowing the night would be fine if he fell asleep after sex. But deprived of his home comforts, he might want to go out, and I felt nervous about him starting a fight. All night I tried to slow things down, knowing that once we'd fucked the frustration would come out. Despite all my efforts, by eleven o'clock we'd already reached the state of clammy postcoital unease, and by 11.20, Paul had decided that enough time had elapsed for his tears not to be taken as a comment on our lovemaking.

I straightened my necklace, adjusting the chain so the pendant sat in the hollow of my collarbone. Paul rolled over to face me, bunching the peach bedsheets as he sobbed. I ran my finger across his forehead, then stroked his cheeks, checking for tears.

'What's wrong?'

He gasped. 'I feel neglected.'

'By me?'

He lay back against the mattress. I felt the weight of the room, wondering if he'd already tried these lines on his wife. The damp sheets smelt more of me than Paul. I wondered if married women could detect that sort of thing.

'What do you think of me, Sarah?'

I smiled at him. 'Don't you know?'

'What would you give me?'

'I give you my body,' I said, softening my voice.

'That's not what I mean.'

'I don't have anything else. I can get money from Henry, tell him it's for me so you don't have to feel ashamed. Maybe my mum could help me out.'

'Not money.'

'What then?'

He paused. 'Can I show you something?'

'Of course.'

Paul sat up, one hand seeking light, the other cigarettes. Iona's ioniser rested on the bedside table, changing the air. I'd never seen one before and worried it was really a miniature spy camera. He walked across to the fitted wardrobe, pushing back the mirrored doors to reveal a row of slack arms and legs, most wrapped in transparent plastic. He reached beneath a pile of jumpers on the upper shelf, then walked back to me.

Kneeling down, he used the small key he'd taken from

the wardrobe to unlock the bedside drawer. There were red marks around the crack of his arse, the hairs there spreading up his lower back. A tube of Calestan, two bagged femidoms and a hardbacked diary. It could be any woman's secret drawer, even mine. Paul took out the book and gave it to me.

'Read this,' he said, 'any page.'

'Paul, I'm not sure . . .'

'Read it.'

Feeling uneasy, I flipped open at the middle. The handwriting was loopy but legible, the blank pages almost entirely filled. I started reading:

> every time I pick up this pen I wish that writing was unnecessary, that Paul's behaviour didn't keep sending me here to pull something out of my wasted life. I have so many thoughts I can't share with him, and I feel more turned on writing my fantasies in here than I ever do when I'm with him. I know I could never be unfaithful, if only because it would prove he's right to be as fucked-up as he is, but every time he touches me I think of the man of my dreams. I sometimes wish I was gay because I'm sure I wouldn't feel guilty if I betrayed him with a woman, but I've never been that keen on oral sex and can't see how it'd be erotic to have a plastic cock strapped onto me or pushed into my privates.

When I looked up, I realised he was watching my face in the mirrored doors.

'Do you feel like that?' he asked.

'About you?'

'About everything. I mean, do you think in that way?'

'I'm not Iona.'

'She's never said any of this to me.'

I read a few more lines, then tried to picture myself

as Paul. I imagined being bent down before the drawer, praying it was empty. And then the bitter gratitude that she'd left words instead of objects. Knowing that opening the diary would change things for ever, and deciding this could be coped with. Then the final, foolish hope that the book would be filled with compliments she'd been too bashful to give him.

'It doesn't say, I mean, she says she's never been . . .'

'Unfaithful? Not according to this.'

'Don't you believe it?'

'Who knows? Maybe she wanted me to find this diary.'

'Come on, Paul. Don't get paranoid. She probably senses you've got someone else and this is her revenge.'

He didn't answer.

'All married people have things they don't tell each other about. How would she feel if she knew about me?' I asked.

'It's not the feelings. It's the dishonesty.'

I laughed, despite myself.

'What's funny?'

'The situation.'

He sat on the edge of the bed. 'Have I ever said anything bad about Iona?'

'No.'

'If she found out I was seeing you, it wouldn't surprise her. I don't disguise my desire for other women. But now I know how Iona really thinks, I can't even look at her.'

'Because of what she's written?'

'Because of what she hasn't said. I wouldn't care if she told me any of that stuff. I want her to be open with me and I'm not squeamish. I love her now more than ever.'

'Okay.'

He looked at me. 'Don't you like it when I say that?'

'I'm just not sure you should talk to me about this. I'm

not going to say what you want to hear. You can't expect me to care about your marriage.'

He took the diary and put it back in the drawer. I knew I'd upset him and wondered why I felt so awkward about this subject. I'm not jealous, and I know the best way to get someone into bed is to talk to them about their girlfriend. Maybe it's the tightness around Paul's lips when he talks about Iona, and my knowledge that this expression is reserved for thinking about his wife.

After the first term's betrayal, I was reluctant to return to university. But my sister persuaded me to see out the year, saying if it didn't work out I could always come home. She was so supportive during those nine months, sending me a letter almost every day. It wasn't until after she'd been hospitalised that I realised she'd written all those words without ever once mentioning how things were going for her.

Paul threw up this morning. He tried to hide the noise by flushing the toilet, but I could hear his gasps above the rumbling water. It was probably nothing, his stomach shrugging off some nasty ingredient in the Pink Champagne, but it added to my sense of Paul's vulnerability at the moment. Usually he escapes all the illnesses that snare the rest of us, proudly tapping his stomach and boasting of his cast-iron guts.

I even considered skipping my afternoon with Henry, the first time I'd ever thought of giving something up for Paul. But I knew it wouldn't be long before he sorted things out with Iona, and it's important to be pragmatic about matters of love.

I waited for Henry outside the town hall, in my usual

place below the sandstone griffin. A woman from the solarium stared out at me. The tinted glass and her heavy tan made her look like a refugee. I know people probably say the same about our place, but I could never work in a tanning shop. They spend all day peeling each other off the electric griddles, memorising the ingredients of cocktails.

Henry arrived at one thirty, with another young woman in tow. She looked like a prostitute, and I felt a quick panic that he had a threesome in mind. This didn't fit with what I knew of Henry, but neither did the state of this girl. Henry gets uneasy if he has a line of dirt under his fingernail and this woman's skin was so pocked and greasy it looked like an unwashed frying pan.

'Sarah, I'd like you to meet my daughter.'

The woman stared at me, then presented her hand at an odd, broken bone angle. I shook it.

'Okay,' said Henry, 'The Wayfarer?'

I shrugged, and we started walking.

We took a window seat. Father and daughter sat opposite me, giving me a chance to check for family resemblance. I knew the girl probably didn't think much of me, in my smart white jacket with three oyster-shaped buttons up each sleeve, but it was impossible to read from her face. Her tiny eyes were almost all pupil, the sockets like pierced holes. Her curly blonde hair looked artificial and bedraggled, as if she'd made a conscious effort to resemble an abandoned doll. The clothes were standard prostitute wear, for Weston at least. Her black tights and neon-purple mini were coupled with an embroidered jumper, the combination a promise of homely rawness.

'What are you having, Sarah?'

I looked at the blackboard behind the till. A waitress took

this as her cue to approach. She waited at the edge of our table, eyes directed downwards.

'Beef, I think. I seem to remember it being nice here.'

Henry patted my hand approvingly, glancing at his daughter. He likes it when I have meat. Most of the women he's been out with in the last five years have been prone to fads. Vegetarianism, dope, strange-coloured hair: habits I have long since left behind.

'Anne-Marie?'

'Just a Coke.'

'You ought to eat something.'

'A Coke'll be fine.'

He didn't argue, maybe because of the way the waitress looked at him. He gave her his order and she left us alone. I knew Henry intended my behaviour to be an example for his daughter, but not what she was supposed to represent to me. Paul's plans are easily guessed and quickly confessed, but Henry's campaigns last for months at a time. He has none of the ease I imagine comes with age and stresses every word as if it is weighted with meaning.

'How's Paul?' he asked.

'Okay.'

'Any new ventures?'

'One.'

He raised his eyebrows. 'Chances of success?'

'Better than usual.'

'So he'll be coming for money.'

'Not this time. I think he'll go for new investors. You know how he feels about borrowing from you.'

'What is it? A restaurant?'

'Nightclub.'

He laughed. 'I wondered when he'd get to that.'

The waitress returned with Anne-Marie's drink, served as always in a heavy glass tumbler. She leaned down to the straw instead of raising it to her mouth. Her lips looked like a plastic smile from a cracker, split in two and stuck to her skin.

Henry showed no interest in Paul's plan. I felt glad I didn't have to talk about it. I knew it would sound stupid to someone as seasoned as Henry, and didn't want to hear why it couldn't work.

Anne-Marie finally gave in and lifted her glass. It occurred to me that Henry might have brought her here to explain himself. *Look at my daughter. Now do you understand why I am with you?* Irritated, I watched his quick eyes, waiting for an expression that would prove my theory.

We finished our meal and separated awkwardly. When Henry and I started seeing each other, I told him that, as a child, whenever I asked my grandfather if I could do something, he'd tease me by saying, 'Not now. *Presently.*' Henry picked up on this, responding to my requests with this hated word. At first I thought it was funny, but now he'd started saying it during sex. As we usually spent our Thursdays in bed together, bringing his daughter today seemed a new method of stalling. Watching Henry and Anne-Marie walk off together, I couldn't help thinking this denial was exciting for him, and resented the waste of my time.

My week is carefully organised to avoid any empty moments, and Henry's premature departure had left me with an afternoon to fill. It was too hot to walk around town so I headed back to the guest house. Sylvia was sitting in the lounge working on her appliqué. She put it down and smiled at me.

'Hello dear.'

'Is it okay if I watch TV with you?'

'Of course,' she said, moving her sewing bag, 'you're just in time for *Countdown*.'

'I'm terrible at quizzes.'

'Nonsense. Anyone can do a quiz. Fetch a piece of paper and we'll play it ourselves.'

I brought the pad from the table and she drew out a scorecard. She turned up the volume. Once we got started, I realised that Sylvia was clearly an old hand at this game, scoring almost as well as the contestants.

'You should go on.'

She laughed, her face pleased. 'I'm sure it's much harder in front of the camera.'

Sylvia scowled when she couldn't get the anagram, and flipped over to the soaps. She seemed pleased to have company, holding my hand and filling me in on the last five years of *Neighbours* and *Home and Away*. Her descriptions were so complex I couldn't believe she got all the information from the programme and imagined her compiling psychological profiles in her head. After the soaps, she stood up and looked at her watch.

'Dinnertime.'

I nodded. 'Thanks for this afternoon, Sylvia.'

'That's okay, dear. I enjoyed myself.'

She smiled again, and left me with the television.

Saturday

Before I met Henry, I made Paul promise that he'd never have sex with Iona and me on the same day. He agreed, and because our relationship was different then, even asked me why. To scare him, I said if he did I'd know, and if I knew, I wouldn't feel the same way. But really I was scared I wouldn't know, and that he could leap from her bed to mine without me realising I was getting the repeat performance.

I remembered this conversation when Paul came over this morning. Not because I thought he was bed-hopping, but because I knew he wasn't. His problems with Iona clearly weren't over, and once again he sought solace with me.

'Why do you sleep so late on Saturdays,' he asked, getting under my duvet. 'You're missing the best part of the day.'

I stared at the wall as he went down on me, still feeling a bit hungover. He always began by lapping my thighs, the sensation reminding me of coming out of the sea and feeling the water trickle down from my swimsuit. When he reached my clit, the dotting pleasure there pulsed with the throbs in my head, the two combining in a delicious neuralgia.

Paul clambered up my body to kiss me, wanting me to feel his wet face and acknowledge his effort. His boyishness chilled me, and I tightened instantly.

'Come now,' he said, rubbing himself against me.

I closed my eyes and thought of Henry, trying to get turned on by imagining them here together, taking it in turns. Sometimes Henry seemed so much sexier than Paul. He'd never be so proud, and hadn't once looked at me as if he wanted to photograph my reactions. I wished for darkness to hide Paul's face, unable to take his triumph today.

'What are you doing this afternoon?' he asked afterwards.

'Maybe some shopping. Why?'

'I wanted to show you something. Up in Sand Bay.'

'Okay,' I agreed, and he patted my leg.

To get to Sand Bay we had to drive along the toll road through Standing Woods. Paul told me to look under the seat for some change. He spoke quickly, his tone almost angry. I took a pound from my purse and gave it to him.

He parked the car in a ditch by a row of thin black bollards, then wiped his forehead and started walking. No tears today. No tenderness either, which was both a surprise and a relief. He could almost be Henry, if I didn't know his silence was only temporary. The hotels here are yellow and brown, as if the bay's name is the literal truth.

The street smelt of hot cars and dead fish. A seagull landed a few metres ahead of me, kicking his feet out like a man falling backwards. Paul stopped by a stone wall filled with finger-sized indentations. I spread my arms along the top of the warmed rock, enjoying the relaxing heat against my face.

'The history of Weston, lesson two,' said Paul, his tone deepening. 'Piers are essential to a pleasure beach, and

Weston is lucky enough to have two. Most people, particularly the tourists, know only of the Grand Pier, with its candy floss and Ghost Train and Bank Holiday punch-ups. But the Grand Pier has a modest sister, known locally, in deference to her sibling, as the Old Pier.'

I looked out across the gelatinous sea to the Old Pier. Its struts and ramps made it look like a spider struggling out of the water.

'Unlike the Grand Pier,' he continued, 'which has always been an attraction in itself, the Old Pier was where people came to get out of Weston. From here the tourists and locals could catch paddle-steamers to Wales or Barry Island.'

'Is it for sale?' I asked, smiling.

'No.'

'No?'

'It's a piece of history. Most of these are in complete disrepair. This one'd cost nothing to fix.'

'And if someone put up this nothing?'

He pushed out his lower lip. 'The owners would be very grateful.'

'Grateful enough to let the restorers suggest a new use for the pier?'

'Maybe. If they came up with something classy.'

I embraced him. He stepped back.

'It's not settled yet. I need investors, contractors, a grant from the lottery.' He looked at me. 'But I have got permission to take the investors inside. Maybe give them a show. What do you think?'

'I think you're brilliant.'

Paul dipped the toe of his shoe into a rock pool and flicked sea water at me.

'This has been a lovely day, Sarah. Thank you.'

'I've enjoyed myself.'

'And the perfect end would be to go for a curry.'
'I've told you. I'm going shopping.'
'That won't take all night.'
'I'm busy tonight.'
'Whatever it is, I'll tape it.'
'I'm going out.'
He stepped up to a higher rock. 'With Henry?'
'With friends.'
'What friends?'
'From the Dolphin.'
'But you hate them.'
'I never said that.'
'Why don't you cancel?' he suggested. 'We could have a lovely curry.'
'No, Paul, I want to go.'
He jumped down onto the sand. 'Well, whatever, but think of me sitting at home while you're out clubbing. Think about what we could have been doing.'
I smiled at him. 'Another night, okay? And I'm really thrilled about the pier.'

Paul let me out by the Conservative Club and I cut through to the shops. Bad timing: the preclosing rush. It's mainly hand-to-hand combat, but pushchairs make useful tanks, their bald generals dribbling and giggling as they lead the charge into enemy legs. The race is on for lager and snacks, everywhere the red-blue skinshirts of the excessively sunburnt. Young marrieds and earnest unemployed hunt for cheap weekend meals, here because it's easier to live in poverty when you've got a beach. Everyone eager for the evening to begin, looking at their watch with every blast from a passing car stereo.
Unsettled by the activity, I headed into the nearest chemist. I always steer clear of the chain stores, their small stock

reminding me of the life I could be enjoying elsewhere. But the local shops are exciting and sexy, a version of the world where the Seventies are held as the zenith of human existence, and elaborate iconostases stand erected to the twin wonders of thighs and eyes.

I found the hairspray I'd come for, and was about to leave when I was distracted by a row of stockings. I still knew my mother's size and her favourite shade, just as I remembered her make-up routine and the letter measurement for her ring finger. I looked at the Pretty Polly woman and lifted her into my basket, approaching the counter to give money for my goddess.

I was to meet the girls by the Grand Central Hotel, beneath the clock that had letters instead of numbers. I hadn't realised how strongly I felt about tonight until Paul asked me to give it up. Amy and Vanessa had never invited me anywhere before, and I felt eager not to scare them away.

I didn't feel hurt that they'd taken so long to approach me. I tended to sleepwalk through my second job, and usually ignored my co-workers' conversation. I'd only started working at the bowling alley to fill my empty evenings, and felt angry at myself now I'd come to rely on the extra money. But that was hardly their fault, and it seemed churlish to turn down the offer of friendship.

I'd anticipated their overture all week, noticing how Amy'd started joining me during every coffee break. I still hadn't said much to Vanessa, but I could tell the older girl liked indulging her friend and had let me come along as a special treat.

Amy arrived at twenty to eight, telling me Vanessa was going to catch up with us when she'd stopped rowing with her boyfriend. Amy's nosering had the odd optical effect of making her face look fat, maybe because this adornment was favoured by all the dumpy girls in Weston.

'Where are we going?'

'My house. Vanessa never goes to pubs on Saturday nights, but I've got a bottle of Archer's we can share.'

'Okay.'

She walked slightly in front of me, looking back as she talked. 'It was really worrying for a moment,' she said, stretching the vowels to increase the suspense, 'my dad had an argument with his girlfriend on the phone and I thought he was going to stay in.'

'Sounds like it's the night for domestic upsets.'

'Did your boyfriend get cross too?'

'A little bit. He wanted to go for a curry.'

'That's not so bad,' she said. 'It's nice to have a boyfriend who wants to take you out. Lee's shouting at Vanessa because he rented a video.'

I laughed.

'Do you usually eat out on a Saturday?' she asked.

'Yeah.'

'Your boyfriend's got money then.'

'He's my boss.'

I could tell from her silence that Amy was impressed, and I felt guilty about showing off.

'No wonder you never come out,' she said. 'Is he married?'

'Yes.'

'Don't you mind?'

'Not really,' I said, enjoying Amy's serious inquiries. 'He's not under my feet all the time.'

'I know what you mean. My ex always wanted to know what I was doing. He thought Vanessa was a bad influence.'

Amy unlocked her front door and we stepped up into the porch. There were several clay owls hooked around the door and I knew instantly that she'd made them. Looking at her again, I noticed how much she resembled the bird, and pictured her painting circles around her eyes.

'I like your owls,' I told her.

She blushed. 'Dad won't let me throw them away. You know how an owl goes twit-twoo?'

'Yeah.'

'Did you know that's really two owls. One going twit and the other going twoo.'

I looked at her. 'That's not true, is it?'

'It is. I saw it on a nature programme.'

She hung up her bag and took off her clogs. The sides of her feet were the shade of pink that always makes me think of nappy rash. I felt self-conscious about removing my own shoes and hoped she wouldn't be cross about me trampling my imprint into her parents' carpet.

'Would you like something to eat? Dad went to the supermarket today.'

'No thanks. I don't feel like eating.'

'Me neither. The alcohol works quicker that way.'

She started cooing to an animal and I prepared myself for the advances of a lolloping dog. But she returned holding a sweet Persian and I allowed myself to stroke it.

'My dad's so proud of this cat. He treats it like a baby.'

We walked through to the lounge. I sat down on the soft brown settee and Amy squatted on the floor, her rump sliding up to reveal the backs of her legs. The decoration reminded me of all the friends' homes I'd visited in adolescence, right down to the horse buckles above the imitation coal-electric fire. I felt embarrassed about being twenty-seven and still sneaking round to someone's house when their parents were out, but once Amy had turned the stereo on and poured us two drinks in tall glasses, I decided to relax and enjoy it.

'How long have your parents been divorced?'

Amy turned towards me. 'They're not divorced.'

'But I thought you said your dad was visiting his girl-friend.'

'He is. We're a pretty liberal family.' She paused. 'No, Mum's dead. Don't worry, it was a long time ago. It sounds sick but I'm glad she's gone. I don't know anyone who understands their dad the way I do.'

I nodded, uncertain what to say. Amy put the frosted glass bottle between her feet and tried to lift it to her lips. I laughed and we smiled at each other, her fat face making me feel happy.

By the time Vanessa arrived we were already halfway through the bottle and Amy made her drink a full glass to catch up. Vanessa was more attractive than Amy, and taller than me. She was wearing an off-white shift dress that complemented her permed black hair. When she raised her arm to knock back the drink, I was amazed at the precision with which she had shaved her armpits, cutting so close that there was no shadow at all.

She didn't say much, and kept looking at me. Amy tried to get us talking, but we were still appraising one another. As touching as Amy's affection was, I knew a friendship with Vanessa would be much more useful. It was a long time since I'd had a genuine female friend, let alone an equal.

Vanessa told a joke about an old man and a nurse, and I made a mental note to pass it on to Henry. The girls filled their glasses the second they finished them, although the alcohol seemed to be having little effect.

'I don't even get hangovers any more,' Amy told me.

Vanessa touched my arm. 'It's like when I was younger. It wasn't serious or anything, but I used to be a little bit anorexic, and if you don't eat for a while, sometimes you stop getting periods. That's what not having hangovers is like. It should be a relief but it's not.'

We finished the bottle and set off for The Princess, Amy's favourite club. Looking at the girls' flushed faces, I realised how long it had been since I'd been excited about a night out. It wasn't as if I wanted to do anything; it was just the freedom of being with people who had no expectations of me.

'How long have you known each other?'

'Best friends since school,' said Amy proudly. 'We tell each other everything.'

Vanessa looked at me. 'There aren't many cool people in Weston Super Mare.'

I linked arms with her. Amy did the same and we marched down the street together, a formidable obstacle.

'We should have names,' said Amy, 'our own secret group.'

Vanessa smiled. 'We are friends, aren't we, Sarah? We're not going to go into work next week and ignore each other.'

I shook my head. 'We're friends.'

'The bowling girls,' said Amy.

'The bowling girls,' we repeated.

It was still warm at nine o'clock and the doormen at The Princess had taken their jackets off. They let us in without paying, telling us we were the first pretty girls they'd seen all evening. Amy went to get some more drinks while we found a table near the dancefloor.

'That's a nice skirt,' Vanessa told me. 'It's like a work skirt, only sexier.'

Two pints and we were up dancing, granted our own space between the men in coloured jackets and the girls in rugby shirts and flat shoes. Amy anchored us, draping her arms across our shoulders. Vanessa offered me a cigarette. I shook my head then took one anyway, wanting to enjoy exactly the same experience as my friends were having.

No one here seemed used to dancing, and the men's hesitant steps suggested they were waiting for someone to laugh at them. Tonight we were all complicit in one enjoyment; a sensation intensified by the way everyone in the club seemed to be wearing the same deodorant, giving off a steady scent that intensified whenever a hot body drew close to me.

Vanessa was moving with her thighs turned outward and her hands moving fast enough to translate the lyrics into sign language. I set myself free from Amy's arms and tried to lose myself in the sway, closing my eyes to the lights and seeing the colours split and dissolve as my ears started to hum. I felt completely at peace and wished that someone would take me down to the beach and throw me into the sea, letting me drown with these beautiful thoughts in my head.

5

Tuesday

Weston was only ever supposed to be the beginning. Before his brain was invaded by nightclub-shaped spaceships, Paul's ambition had always been to expand his operation into other resorts. Although many of the main markets were already overcrowded, there were still plenty of places worth exploring. Minehead, for instance. Lynton and Lynmouth. Burnham-on-Sea. But the most obvious target for our attentions was Clevedon, Weston's sleepy sister. Not only was it the perfect size, but Paul already had a contact there in the form of Jodie Lace, an old London crony who'd previously expressed enthusiasm about our neon displays.

Until now, Paul had always seemed reluctant to follow this up. It was his insurance policy, the diamond in his back pocket he didn't want valued. But coming up with the nightclub plan had filled him with fresh confidence, and any possibility of finding more money had to be followed up. So now the four of us were driving over for a talk with Jodie, and the opportunity to discuss March Entertainments' next step.

Mum told me about Melissa. I wouldn't have opened the letter if I'd known it was from her. Their handwriting's so similar, and it'd been at least two days since my sister had contacted me. The moment I read what had happened to her I decided I had to drop out of university. I felt convinced it was my fault. Melissa'd put so much effort into supporting me that she had no energy left for herself. I called Mum and told her I'd be on the next train.

All the way home I wondered what might have happened to prompt Melissa's breakdown. I prayed her depression had been brought on by Mum, A-Level pressure, or trouble with friends. Anything as long as it wasn't me.

I hate cars. Particularly full ones. Four bodies in that tiny space, all fiddling, tapping, twitching. I hate the sensation of someone sitting behind me, and always avoid the cinema and theatre. Pubs and clubs I can cope with, as long as there's room to move. The only confinement I enjoy is sharing a single bed, which seems much more significant than being sprawled across a messy double.

Neil seemed particularly unsuited to sitting still, and I could hear him chewing and shuffling about. His fidgeting is irritating, but nowhere near as creepy as his absolute stillness when anyone speaks to him, mouth freezing even in midchew.

'So what sweets did you get?' Paul asked.

'Flying Saucers,' Neil replied.

'Great. A mouthful of dust in a cardboard pouch. Mary?'

'Barley sugars.'

'Grandmother's favourite. Just don't make yourselves sick,' he told them, his tone indulgent.

'Did you have a good weekend, Mary?' I asked.

Mary leaned forward. 'Excellent. I went out on my own and I met these two guys who were going to a party in Bath.

They drove me there in their van, but I didn't know anyone and it turned into this weird sex thing so I just walked out. I spent all night exploring the city and in the morning I caught the first bus home.'

She directed all this to Paul and I felt a twinge of my previous annoyance with her. I wanted my lover to put her down but he didn't say anything, staring at the road. I knew Mary wasn't his type, but resented the way she tried to make herself sound like she was some wild streetchild, especially when I could tell her family were far wealthier than mine. It worried me that he might go to her for variety, pleased he could pull someone so different from himself.

'What about you, Neil?'

'I don't know anyone to go out with.'

'Get Sarah to take you,' said Paul. 'She's a real one for the clubs.'

'Only The Princess. Paul's exaggerating.'

'I haven't been there,' Mary said. 'Would you let me come one evening?'

Paul smiled at me.

'Sure,' I told her, 'although it might be a bit small for you.'

'Don't worry,' she said, 'I like anywhere with loud music.'

Neil walked alongside me. Paul thought the four of us trooping in together would look amateur, and amazingly, assigned the task to me and Neil. While we were talking to Jodie, he would take Mary on a research mission, checking out the pubs and arcades. Being alone with Neil made me feel exposed, stripped of my usual safety. It's his energy that scares me, the limber boybody beneath his charcoal suit.

Jodie's office was above an estate agents'. Framed menus hung on the walls of the reception area, some with signatures, some without. They looked like diplomas, or the recommendation letters Paul has. The austere decor seemed better suited to an insurance agency.

'Sarah Patton and Neil Renard,' I told the temporary girl, 'from March Entertainments.'

She repeated this into the intercom.

We waited. Then she said: 'Ms Lace understood she'd be talking to a Mr March.'

'We're representatives of his,' I told her. 'Paul thought Ms Lace would prefer to speak to us.'

She gave Jodie this information, then said: 'Ms Lace has some business to complete before she speaks to you. If you'll take a seat she'll be with you in five minutes.'

It occurred to me that Paul might have engineered this to belittle my authority in front of Neil. Revenge for my snubbing him on Saturday night. I tried to seem unconcerned by the wait, but hated the idea that Neil and Paul might get together later to laugh at me.

Jodie came into the reception. A slightly overweight woman with a flushed face, she dressed casually, wearing blue jeans and a peach blouse. The moment I saw her I realised Paul's wisdom in sending Neil, knowing my role was to watch and keep quiet.

'So,' she said to Neil, 'tell me about your displays.'

Neil caught my eye, then smiled at Jodie. He understood too, and I knew he'd enjoy flirting with her.

'At the moment we've got four basic models. Thirty-two, sixty-four and one hundred and twenty-eight characters in red, or sixty-four in green.'

'Do you have any with you?'

He turned to me. 'Has Paul got one in the car?'

'I would have thought so,' I said. 'You never know when you're going to meet a prospective customer.'

'My sentiments exactly,' said Jodie. 'My biggest coup happened when I went to the States on holiday. I was sitting next to this little American couple on the flight over, and we got talking and it turned out they had this whole chain of restaurants and they had me back across for four weeks of promotions advice.'

I was distracted from the career woman in front of me by the party girl behind her. The party girl was tanned and smiling, moving between nightclubs and the beach in a series of photographs stuck behind a layer of glass. It seemed odd that Jodie was prepared to show off her holiday snaps to her clients, and I wondered if the thin woman behind her was Jodie's temporary girl.

'Anyway, the market here,' continued the career woman, 'is best at the top end. Most of the business in Weston are inherited concerns, and because Clevedon is the way it is they don't have to worry about competition. But certainly among my associates, a neon display would seem a worthwhile investment.'

Jodie seemed to switch off the moment she started speaking, our conversation boring her even before it began. I could see Neil felt scared he was screwing this up, so I said to her: 'What about the rest of our operation?'

'What about it?'

'That inherited concern thing. Is that your way of warning us off your territory?'

She laughed. 'How much do you know about me and Paul?'

'I know he sees you as a useful contact.'

'I owe everything to Paul. When he had money he helped me a hundred times. And if he wants to move his business into Clevedon, I'll be happy to help. But you have to understand what I'm telling you. People in Clevedon don't get intimidated that easily.'

'We're not in the business of intimidating people.'

She stared at me. 'Of course not.'

We were supposed to meet Paul and Mary outside Clevedon Amusements, but we arrived early and decided to kill the time inside.

Amusements. It sounded so quaint. In Weston, it was always arcades. Giant hammers to hit pink blobs popping up from cushioned holes. Life-sized motorbikes lined up in rows of five. One pound the minimum stake. Here one-armed bandits still reigned supreme, and five pounds lasted five hours instead of five spins.

'Air hockey?' suggested Neil.

'I'd prefer a game of pool.'

'No table. Come on. Air hockey.'

I stroked my fingers across the metal surface, feeling the air come through the tiny holes. I remembered how terrified I'd been in infant school when a teacher told me skin was full of holes, then tried to concentrate on the tingling sensation instead. Neil placed a puck on the table and whacked it with his plastic handgrip.

'She was a bitch, wasn't she?'

'That didn't stop her fancying you.'

I waited for a retort, but he kept quiet, staring down at the table while a blush spread across his cheeks. I was surprised at how able he was, bouncing the puck off every side of the table before knocking it through my goal. But I'd known boys like him before, adept at only the most trivial challenges. I tried to mirror his confident stance, but the speed and consistency of his attacks defeated me.

After the air hockey, we played a few games of pinball and I managed to regain some dignity. I find it easier to concentrate on a bouncing ball than a spinning puck, and the pace of pinball agrees with me. My favourite part is the dead moments when the ball is coming down towards the chute and there's no way of changing its trajectory.

I sensed Paul come up behind me, then felt his hands on my waist. I felt surprised at such intimacy in front of Neil and Mary, and wondered if his gesture was a warning to Neil. I felt depressed my lover didn't know me better. Even if I hadn't long since sworn off younger men, Neil had little to interest me.

'So this is how you spend company time, is it?' he asked, laughing.

To prove he was a good sport, Paul permitted one game of table football before we went home. We played doubles, boys against girls. They defeated us easily, Mary too nervous with the goalkeeper to block their shots.

We dropped off Neil and Mary and Paul drove to the lock-up at the back of the office. I'd got so used to making love in a bed that it seemed odd to return to our past privation. I was going to tell him to drive over to Sylvia's, but I sensed he'd brought me here for a reason and would be disappointed if I made a fuss.

'I've wanted you all day,' he said, gripping my leg. He smiled eagerly, winding back my chair's plastic cog until I lay horizontal. He started unbuckling his trousers, then looked at me and opened the car door instead. I raised myself up to watch as he walked to a white metal box in the corner of the garage. I'd didn't know if it was good or bad that I'd never noticed the box before. He rooted around inside it, then returned with four bikechains and an orange cloth.

He opened the door and pulled my legs straight. I don't often wear stockings and Paul sighed as he stroked the straps and touched my thighs. Then tugged down my fawn French knickers and pushed up my pale skirt. My calves tingled after the long drive and I twisted back and forth as he chained my ankles to the steering wheel. His breathing became more ragged as he moved up to truss me to the seatbelt. He held the orange cloth in front of my face and I had a sudden, ridiculous fear that he was going to kill me. He stretched the cloth into a thin gag and tied it round my mouth. The material had the faint odour of petrol and I concentrated on keeping my tongue away from it.

He unzipped his trousers and lowered himself onto me. I'd always been able to trust his touch before, but today his fingering felt adolescent and fiddly, as if Neil's digits had been grafted onto Paul's hands. The only reassurance came from the familiar heat of his groin. Turning his head away from my eyes, he held me open and tried to push his cock inside me. I grimaced. No one noticed.

His movements were harder than usual, a rough force tearing at me. I felt tears coming and held my head still to stop them escaping and leaving a trace. Paul murmured to himself as he thrust. It seemed important that I should know what he was saying, but the words remained just inaudible. I tried to move my hips to better receive his arcs, but his weight kept forcing me back down. It took two minutes of motion before I felt any pleasure, and then it was both more intimate and more distant than usual, a heavy, muffled sensation like being rubbed up through my skirt.

He looked up at me when he came, his eyes scaring me. I was used to hunger, need, even hatred. But Paul's face showed bright innocence. His pupils rolled right up, then he snapped back and gave me loads of little kisses, his damp lips moving over my face and eyes. I tried to look happy but the gag's scent had made me woozy and I fell back, hanging limp in my tethers.

I felt his wetness ooze out with him, and he bent down to release my legs. He rubbed my muscles carefully, squeezing my calves where the cramp had set in. Then he freed my mouth and unlocked the chains that held my hands. He kissed my neck and breastbone and wound my chair back to its original position. The felt carseat prickled against my backside and I wondered how he'd explain the stiffened fur to Iona.

'That was okay, wasn't it?' he asked.

'Of course.'

He stared at me. I felt guilty, worried I hadn't shown enough enthusiasm. He nodded and turned away, starting the engine. I knew he was angry with me, but couldn't see any way to talk about it. The car reversed out of the lock-up and swung round onto the quiet evening road. I rescued my underwear but didn't put it on, worried I'd offend him further. He stopped the car outside Sylvia's.

'Well, goodnight,' I said.

He swallowed. 'You're a hard woman, Sarah.'

'What?' I asked.

'You're hard. That's all.'

I knew better than to say anything. Paul'd been up and down for weeks now, and he'd probably apologise tomorrow. I kissed his cheek and left him to his misery.

5

Thursday

Sand is the enemy in a seaside town, and the streets of Weston are filled with red-eyed strangers, as if the place is permanently playing host to a lonely hearts convention. Even if it doesn't sting your eyes, sand will soon turn up in your bed and underwear, beneath your toenails and between your teeth.

I was watching the sand make yellow squiggles on the pavement when Henry's feet scuffed up a fresh cloud.

'Where do you want to eat today?' he asked, sitting on the bench beside me.

'Do you mind if we go for a walk first?'

'Not at all. Where to?'

'Just along the beach.'

He smiled and pulled a stray hair from my lip. 'You're getting quite sentimental about this place, aren't you?'

We walked past the 1905 building and the Shellfish Bar. He'd made an effort today, and I wondered if he'd started wanting me again. I smiled at Henry and stroked his face, letting him know I preferred his oiled hair and pressed waistcoat to his recent dishabille.

'I'm glad you came,' I told him. 'There was a weird guy taking photographs.'

'Of you?'

'Of nothing. It wasn't like he was looking for good views or anything. Just walls and bits of pavement.'

Henry nodded. 'He's called Christian. He used to be a friend of mine. It's all rather sad really.'

'What's wrong with him?'

'He's not mad,' Henry told me. 'It used to be his job.'

'Taking pictures of nothing?'

He laughed. 'Christian had the best job in England. Covering beauty contests for the *Picture Post*.'

He jumped down from the pavement to the beach, then lent me his support as I followed him. Further out towards the sea tractors were making double tori in the thick brown sand. The tracks reminded me of my sister's habit of scratching her nails across the back of chocolate bars.

'Completely the wrong sort of person for the task, of course,' he continued. 'He didn't get any enjoyment from it at all. Saw it as this big aesthetic challenge. See it however you like, I told him. Just let me look at the pictures.'

'How'd you meet him?' I asked.

'He was a friend of the family. Things were different then. Your father'd get drunk with someone else's father and then the boy'd be round your house every second Saturday. I was ghastly to him, but he admired me because I was older. Miss Weston was coming up at what's now the Playhouse and I asked him if he had any spare tickets. He gave me five. I got free beer all week. Miss Weston was the *ne plus ultra* of beauty shows, and my friends couldn't believe they'd be going.

'They had a name comedian, I forget who, and singers and dancers and everything. We spent all week getting ready for it. We hired dress suits and bought new shoes. They were grand seats too, right up the front.'

I stopped to take off my shoes. We'd walked out past the tractors to the sea. It wasn't healthy to walk through the water, but I was more afraid of sandworms than sewage, and as I couldn't see any evidence of their presence, I was happy to let the chocolate foam splash over my toes.

'The girls came out,' Henry continued, 'and I settled on mine straight away. Number five. I knew the others would laugh at my choice, but to me number five was perfect. She had lovely brown hair, pinned up, but with loose bits over her shoulders. She wore black velvet gloves and she had a really nice tentative smile.

'She was all nervous, and seemed unsure about what she was doing there. That did it for me. I can't stand too much confidence in a woman. The other girls all acted as if they didn't care if they won, but you just knew they'd be heartbroken when they lost. No, number five was my girl, even though I knew she'd never win.'

I noticed a set of footprints running along the sand beside me. They were incredibly slim indentations, almost like exclamation marks. I wondered who would wear shoes like that so close to the sea, and then pictured Henry's beauty queen, traipsing across the beach in evening wear.

'In the interval I met up with the others and asked them who they'd gone for. Number five. Number five. Number five. We'd all gone for the same girl. Maybe it was because we thought we had a chance with her because she was less intimidating than the rest. But one thing was certain, if we'd all gone for her there was no way she was going to win.'

He brushed a fly away from his face. 'That's right, isn't it? In these beauty contests there's always one girl who's clearly the best looking and she never comes home with the prize.'

The flies were bothering me now, and I decided to move back towards the beach until we got past the largest clumps of seaweed. Henry put his arm around me, stroking my bare shoulder. Even after all this time I still feel excited when he does things like that in public.

'Julie Shaw, she was called. She wasn't just good looking, she was witty too. Definitely the cleverest in that section where the girls tell the audience about themselves. All in all, she was as close as you can get to perfection in a woman.'

He belched. 'I'm sorry. Excuse me,' he said, taking a packet of indigestion tablets from his pocket. 'I think my stomach's trying to tell me something.'

'Do you want to turn back?' I asked, used to this routine.

'Would you mind? I'm sorry. It must be a real burden to you.'

'It's fine,' I told him. 'Carry on with the story.'

'Well, after all that, she won. I couldn't believe it. Somehow this creature, who wasn't obvious at all, seduced the entire auditorium. The audience was applauding forever. And we could all see Christian up on stage, photographing Julie with her tiara and flowers.'

I didn't mind curtailing our stroll, but the speed with which Henry was heading back irritated me, cutting straight up the beach, and ruining the relaxed mood I'd settled into.

'We all dreamt about Julie that night. She really was Miss Weston if you know what I mean. It was the first time I'd understood how a person could represent a place. Julie was the kind of woman who would look equally at home in a launderette or on the silver screen. We all bought copies of the next *Picture Post* and taped her picture to the headboards of our beds.

'If she'd really been our angel, Julie would have disappeared after that one incredible night. And for a while, it seemed as if we would never see her again. After all, the future careers of most beauty queens only last until they pass on their tiaras to their successors. But Christian had been seriously taken with Miss Weston and he persuaded the *Post* to do a follow-up spread with her posing on the sand.

'Christian tipped us off and we went down to the front to sit in deck chairs and watch. I'd been reading an interview with a film star in a movie magazine who said that glamorous women were usually lonely because men were too intimidated to approach them. I was convinced this was the case with Julie and decided I'd approach her as if she was any other girl on the beach.

'But at the end of the shoot, Julie kissed Christian. Now you've got to understand that Christian had never shown any interest in women before. In fact, we thought he was a closet queer and they'd only employed him because they knew he wouldn't try anything with the models. Plus he was a pretty odd-looking man, nearly seven feet tall with almost albino colouring. So it seemed most likely that this was just a model's way of thanking her photographer for making her look good. But after the kiss they put their arms around each other and walked off holding hands.'

He stopped talking until we reached The Wayfarer, and I asked Henry if we could get a window seat, wanting to still feel the heat from the sun.

'Beef?' he asked.

'Of course.'

I recognised the waitress from our last visit with Anne-Marie. I tried to smile knowingly at her, but she ignored me and looked at Henry.

The waitress took down our orders and returned to the kitchen. By the end of the month, everyone knew about Christian and Julie. His mother was delighted, assuring everyone that her future daughter-in-law was everso down-to-earth.

'It probably sounds seedy to you, a photographer and his model falling in love. But things were different then, and

Christian was too sincere to exploit anyone. Once they'd got together, Christian gave up the magazine job and found Julie an agent. Then they drew up a contract which stipulated that Christian was to be Julie's personal photographer, and they started selling the pictures all around the world.

'For three years, success followed success. Then the agent arranged to take Julie up to London for a screen test with a friend in the business. He also made her promise not to tell Christian. But because Julie loved her husband so much, and had seen no evidence that he wanted anything but the best for her, she was unable to keep her word.

'Christian, of course, was furious. He was convinced the agent wanted Julie to sleep with the producer and forbad her from going. I remember Julie in tears, years later, when she told me how grateful she was to her husband for saving her from that humiliation.

'Together, Christian and Julie came up with the ideal revenge against the agent for trying to break up their happy marriage. From then on, every photo shoot would have some grotesque detail that would make it impossible for him to sell the pictures. Julie would smear her make-up or open her eyes and lips too wide. Christian would juxtapose her body with inappropriate scenery, a sewer outlet or a naked child on the beach. Eventually the agent gave in and dissolved the contract.

'After that, Christian and Julie set about rebuilding her career. But Julie was getting on, and the year of weird photos was hard to shake off. And although Christian did everything he could to make his wife look beautiful, the pictures were forced and terrifying, as if Julie was going to break out of the frame and smother the observer to death.'

The waitress returned with our meals. She set down the two plates of beef, then went to get Henry his whisky and ginger ale. Henry cut up his meat, leaned forward, and continued: 'Before long, Christian realised he wasn't going to sell any more pictures of Julie. He got his old job back at the magazine and started working with new models. But in order to keep Julie happy they carried on doing photo shoots and Christian made mock-up calendars with his wife's picture replacing one of the real girls.

'Even in her fifties, Julie continued to pose for Christian, and taking photographs remained as integral to their romance as kissing or making love.

'I hadn't spoken to Christian for years and was amazed when he came down to the arcade to invite me to dinner. Years before I would have refused immediately, but as you get older anyone you've known for more than a decade becomes a close friend. And I suppose I still had a crush on Julie, even after all this time. So I went to their house and Julie made a huge meal and they both drank a lot. At the end of the evening Christian took me into the study and handed me an envelope.

'Christian had decided he would relaunch Julie's career by doing some nudie shots for the girlie mags. I was the first person he'd shown the pictures, and if I thought they were good enough he was going to send them to *Health and Efficiency*. Of course, it's impossible to tell a man you're unaroused by pictures of his naked wife, so I smiled and said they were hot stuff.

'Three weeks later, Julie committed suicide. It was a Hollywood-style death, booze and sleeping pills. Probably the most glamorous thing she ever did. But the most revealing detail was never made public. A friend of a friend was a coroner who witnessed the autopsy and he told me that inside Julie's stomach, as well as the booze and the pills, they found the chewed up remains of six lipsticks, a powder brush, and the broken glass of a compact mirror.'

Henry sat back, lifting another forkful of beef and peas into his mouth. As I watched him eat, I thought about

Christian still taking photos of the places where his wife had once stood. If I saw him again I would ask him if he could make one of the pictures into a postcard so that I could send it to Charlie, an old boyfriend of mine. Henry's story reminded me of being nine years old and my grandfather telling me that he didn't want to marry again because he didn't want two women waiting for him in Heaven. That kind of romance seemed long gone, and although Henry had presented Julie's tale as a tragedy, I'd happily trade her life for mine.

5

Friday

Paul showed me the plans this morning. I don't know whether he'd had them done professionally or given the job to a creative mate, but either way they looked excellent. The designer had allowed himself little sc-fi flourishes which could, I suppose, be the mark of an amateur, but I took them as the self-deprecating confidence of a serious technical artist.

'So,' Paul said, 'what do you think?'

'They're good.'

'You don't like them.'

'I do. They're excellent.'

'No, something's wrong.' He looked nervous. 'Tell me and I'll change it. I really want your input on this.'

I sucked in my lips, embarrassed that I was being so sentimental. 'It's not the plans.'

'What then?'

'I didn't think you'd get started so quickly.'

'But that's good, isn't it? Why does that upset you?'

My feet squirmed. 'I thought this was our thing.'

'It is. That's why I want to get started.'

'But I liked it being a fantasy. It feels like it's becoming real too quickly.'

He tried to hide his smile. 'This isn't like you, Sarah.'

'I know. I'm being silly. The plans are great.'

'It's still a long way off, you know. There's plenty of time for fantasising. Besides, you thought I'd bought the pier the first time we went there.'

'Just ignore me. I'm really proud of you.'

He stared at me. 'I'm doing this for you, Sarah. I want to give you something back.'

I hugged him. He shuffled the plans together and put them back in the drawer. Neil tapped on the door.

'Jodie Lace is on the phone.'

'Okay,' he said, returning to his desk. 'Thanks, Sarah.'

I left him to his call.

I really didn't feel in the mood for the bowling alley tonight. Fridays are the worst shift anyway, especially after a hectic week. I hate beginning my weekend with a night behind the counter. I used to think I'd never get used to working here, but nowadays I'm so tired I hardly notice it. Only in headaches do I hear the skid and clatter of bowling balls, only in dreams do I register the specific *chunk* of the machine that sets up pins. Even the odour of the shoes is no longer oppressive, and I can almost recognise each pair from their scent.

My shift lasts four hours. I've learnt how to measure this time without a watch and now deliberately leave mine at home. The first two hours are the busiest, with families wanting to entertain their kids and get them home before the scuffles begin. Amy's a good person to work with, even-tempered at our busiest moments.

Our supervisor prefers the evenings when Vanessa doesn't come in. He's scared of her and knows she'll come up with a sarcastic retort to any request. Vanessa uses this to keep him away from us, increasing the boredom of his already lonely night. I think Adrian would like to see Vanessa sacked, but as the owners of the alley always stop to talk to her whenever they visit, he thinks she's a relative of theirs, a misconception we all encourage.

Adrian doesn't seem to realise his ginger hair is unattractive, allowing it to make a guest appearance on his chin. He is, however, the only person who looks good in the red and brown uniform, and when I first arrived he did make sure I had enough money to live on until my first wage cheque.

'Vanessa's asked me to test your loyalty,' said Amy.

I looked at her.

'You haven't forgotten your promise, have you?' she asked. 'You said you were our friend.'

'I am your friend.'

'Vanessa needs you to do her a favour. She's got a problem with Lee.'

'What sort of problem?'

'She won't say. But she's coming to the alley after you finish tonight.'

Amy smiled at me and walked across to the lanes. I felt irritated that Vanessa'd sent Amy to talk to me, and wondered if this was a test. I wanted these girls as friends, but this sudden need for commitment made me uneasy.

Still, at least it gave me something new to worry about. I'd spent all week stressing about Henry and Paul, and felt eager to cast them from my mind. I just couldn't help wondering if it was something I'd done that made them both go strange at the same time. After Henry's story yesterday, neither of us felt like going back to his room, which made it over a month since we'd last made love. And Paul's behaviour today didn't make any sense coming after our adventure in the lock-up. It felt like Henry and Paul were forcing themselves to associate me with their most extreme emotions, as if they needed to believe that getting rid of me would purge them of everything they felt guilty about. I wanted to remind them of when I was just a stranger with a provocative smile, and all my body made them think about was no-strings sex.

Adrian approached me. 'I'm going to work through my break. I can handle the till but I need you to do the lanes.'

'No problem.'

'Good.'

'So what's wrong?' I asked Vanessa.

'Nothing,' she told me, 'but Lee's got himself into this thing, and it's the sort of thing where I need to be there, but I can't go alone. You won't have to do anything.'

'I'm pretty tired,' I told her. 'It's been a long day.'

'It'll only take half an hour. I'd go with Amy but she's too wishy-washy.'

We met Lee at the back of the Buzz. He stood below the disco's flashing red sign, talking to a doorman. He bounced his shoulder against the wall as he spoke, neck pressed into the collar of his green leather jacket. He noticed us and walked across, pausing to light a cigarette.

'Is this Sarah?' he asked.

I nodded.

'I'm Lee,' he said, offering his hand.

'Hi.'

He turned to Vanessa. 'Are we ready?'

'I think so.'

Lee put his arm around Vanessa's broad back. They looked good together, reminding me of couples I'd envied in school. I didn't know where we were going and didn't like to ask. I walked alongside Vanessa, stepping down into the gutter whenever a nightstroller needed to pass.

'I really appreciate your assistance tonight, Sarah,' Lee told me. 'You're a good friend to Vanessa.'

I had to wait until Vanessa looked away to properly appraise Lee. He was wearing a yellow T-shirt and black jeans, black hair shaved at the sides and curly on top. His body seemed a little runtish, but only because Vanessa looked so strong.

I thought about Vanessa's friendship with Amy and realised if I'd grown up with these two girls, I'd always feel unsatisfied when alone with Amy, knowing that whatever Vanessa was doing she'd be having the better time. And if I was with Vanessa, I'd know we were enjoying the greatest evening ever, and look forward to telling Amy about all the fun we had when she wasn't there.

There were more people once we reached the Sea Front, voices and laughter taking the edge off the darkness. Cars tooted as they careered round the tourist information centre, the first stage in the boy-racer circuit. I felt safer now we were out of the backstreets, but couldn't help worrying about walking home when this was finished.

A girl in a black dress pushed past me, then called to her friends. They headed towards a man selling neon necklaces from a plastic coolbox. Previous customers trailed into the distance, bobbing like luminous buoys in a pale-orange sea. I smiled at Vanessa, remembering how I bought a necklace on my first night here alone, three years before. Coming down to the beach at midnight to make the place my own, the plastic band (which later split and dribbled toxic liquid down my neck) had seemed an essential purchase, proof I had no snobbery about the Weston spirit.

Wearing my new necklace, I'd walked out towards the sea. Ahead of me, I picked out a black shape in the darkness. It looked like an animal that had fallen over and got stuck in the mud. Its breathing sounded strained, and I wondered if it was still alive. But as I walked closer I realised it was not one body but two, and to go any further would disturb them. As my eyes became accustomed to the darkness, I noticed more and more of these black shapes, each one only a few metres from the next. It was like looking for insects in a layer of silt, watching as each shadow wriggled into life.

I felt compromised by my discovery, especially as I'd lost my virginity on a beach. It happened on holiday in Exmouth, the day after my sister lost hers. My date had taken me to a fairground, then on to a disco. He'd had his picture taken with a bunny girl and we danced to Soft Cell and The Human League. My sister was there with his friend, who'd brought some poppers and speed. We did the speed in the club and took the poppers to the beach with us.

I don't remember his body but I remember his clothes. He was wearing black leather boots with pointed silver toecaps that he worried would rust in the wet sand. He had soft black trousers that didn't chafe my legs when he pulled them down to fuck me. Most of all, I remember his shirt. Thin and cream coloured, with a black roman numeral print. I tugged and tugged at his shirt until he told me to stop trying to tear it.

Vanessa stopped. 'Are you sure about going alone, Lee? He's bound to have people with him.'

'I'm not alone,' he said. 'Besides, if I don't sort it out now, the threat's always going to be hanging over me. I like living in Weston. I don't want to have to be prepared for a fight every time I go out.'

He walked towards the pier. Vanessa took off her shoes and turned to me. 'Bit of climbing needed here, Sarah.'

I watched Lee scale a wooden strut just beyond the locked gates. Vanessa padded out into the damp sand and went after him, her climbing technique favouring her thighs over her arms. I looked up at her tight buttocks and pulled myself up onto the strut, trying not to tear my trousers on the sharp bolts. I felt the breeze against my face and looked out towards the muddy banks, remembering how my sister and I tried to walk all the way round the pier when the tide was out. Vanessa reached down and hoisted me up onto the pier. She was out of breath and I could tell she wanted me to share in her excitement.

Up on the pier, I began to feel nervous, thinking that whoever was after Lee wouldn't worry about attacking me as well. If the fight was taking place in a backstreet or a lock-up, it'd be easy to pretend I wasn't involved. But coming here seemed an unnecessary risk, especially as I had no idea what Lee was fighting about. After all, I hardly knew Vanessa, and she said she'd chosen me because I wasn't wishy-washy. Fifteen minutes ago that sounded flattering. Now I worried what would be expected of me.

At the end of the pier, there were three orange tips in the shelter and two by the arcade. Up against five. Okay. Lee took his own cigarettes from his pocket, lighting three at once and handing two to Vanessa and me.

'About time,' said a man by the arcade.

Lee kissed Vanessa and walked towards the men. One of them came forward and they both dropped their cigarettes before Lee swung at him. He missed, and before he had time for a second attempt, his opponent moved closer and appeared to be bundling Lee up in his arms. I couldn't tell what was happening until the man managed to pull Lee to the floor. But he seemed to misjudge it and Lee ended up on top of him, his black hair glistening as he punched the man in face. A second man moved in and dropped down on both of them, then pushed himself up so he could punch Lee in the back. Until this point the blows had been obscured and apart from a sense of concern that this was happening, I'd been unaffected by the fight. Now I could see the results of the violence I felt sick and upset, wanting them to stop but knowing I couldn't intervene.

The man punched Lee with both hands, his fingers knitted together as if he was trying to resuscitate him. I watched the joined fists come down six times, knocking groans from Lee's chest and squashing him onto the first man. The fight seemed unfair and I looked at Vanessa. She was watching without comment, the cigarette moving away from and back to her lips. Lee tried to swivel round, but after every movement, the second man knocked him back to inaction. When Lee stopped moving, the second man pushed him from his friend and onto the rough wooden boards of the pier. The first man stood up and gave Lee a final kick. Then he walked over to us and said: 'You're good girls. You know how to watch a fight.'

He stared at Vanessa and seemed about to kiss her. I wondered what she would do if he did. But after his stare, he turned round and the two men walked back down the pier. Only then did Vanessa go to her boyfriend's aid, lifting him up from the boards and putting her arms around him. I walked behind the couple, looking over Vanessa's shoulder at Lee's face, wanting to know how badly he'd been hurt.

Vanessa spat on a tissue and wiped it across Lee's face, but there was no blood there. Lee lay still in her arms, and she put her finger between his lips, running it across his gums and teeth. Then she tried to get him up on his feet, gesturing to me to support her.

'Come on, Lee,' she said, 'let us take your weight.'

'I'm sorry,' he said. 'Don't tell anyone about this.'

The orange tips still glowed in the shelter, and I felt unnerved that the strangers had observed the fight without comment. We helped Lee back along the pier, until halfway down when he released himself from our grip and walked alone.

'Do you want to come back for a drink, Sarah?' Vanessa asked.

'I'm really tired,' I insisted.

'Come on, Sarah,' Lee said, 'after all that you've got to let us thank you.'

Lee and Vanessa shared a flat in Sand Bay. The rooms were small but every powerpoint was connected to a four-socket adapter, black wires trailing across the thick carpets. On every surface there was a blinking 00:00, and the range of equipment easily rivalled Paul's place. The moment we were inside Vanessa selected CDs for the five-disc carousel and Lee went to the fridge.

'What would you like, Sarah?'

'A beer,' I said, 'I don't mind which brand.'

There were three large cushions on the floor. We took one each. Vanessa began rolling a joint on the low coffee table. Lee handed me a beer, and I felt envious of the obvious comfort of their living arrangement. Vanessa removed her shoes and thrust her sandy feet into her boyfriend's lap, demanding a massage. He started squeezing and stroking, saying: 'At least it's over.'

'You did well,' Vanessa told him. 'It took guts to go up there without back-up.'

'She's only being nice to me because you're here,' Lee told me. 'She wants you to think she's nice. If you weren't here, she'd be calling me a baby.'

'That's because if Sarah wasn't here, you'd be crying and rolling around in pain.'

Vanessa finished the joint and held it up for Lee's inspection. He smiled at her.

'I'm getting better, aren't I?'

'Vanessa used to be crap at rolling joints,' Lee told me.

'I never had to roll them before,' she said. 'My old boyfriends were gentlemen.'

'Suckers, more like,' Lee said. 'There are two skills the

perfect girlfriend should never be without. Rolling joints and giving blow jobs.'

'I give excellent blow jobs,' Vanessa replied, 'just not to you.'

'That's not funny.'

'You didn't appreciate me. I had to take my talents elsewhere.'

'That's really not funny.'

'Come on, Lee,' she said, 'you know I'm all yours.'

Lee offered to walk me home but I said I'd be okay. I could tell he was trying to make Vanessa jealous, and I didn't want her thinking of me as a rival. I'd hardly spoken to her tonight, but no doubt Amy'd passed on the secrets I'd shared last Saturday, and any woman who can seduce her boss is not to be trusted.

'You sure you're going to be all right?' Lee asked one last time.

'Of course. Goodnight, Lee.'

'Goodnight.'

5

Saturday

I was still dreaming when someone sat on my bed. The gentle droop of the mattress made me think I'd been sent home in my sleep, just in time for one of those Saturday mornings when my mum tried to work out what I'd been up to. Instinctively, I pulled my feet out of reach, embarrassed about my happy naked warmth and unable to shake the groundless fear that my covers were about to be whipped back.

Waking up and seeing Sylvia's shoulders made me feel even more nervous, worried she'd come upstairs to kick me out. I attracted her attention with an experimental snuffle, and she handed me an envelope.

'This arrived for you.' She waited while I checked the handwriting. 'Which one of your suitors is it from?'

'Neither. It's from Mum.'

'That's nice.'

She looked back to the door, avoiding my eyes. I rarely got personal letters, but I knew Sylvia had other reasons for entering my room. I stared at the nape of her neck, waiting for her to speak.

'Sarah,' she began, 'you know I think of you as more than just a guest.'

'Yeah,' I said quietly.

'I mean, I like my guests. I know their names and their children's names and look forward to seeing the ones who return every year, but I think of you as a someone special.'

'I'm glad.'

'And,' she said, finally looking at me, 'I'm worried about you. I know you're an intensely private person and this is probably completely the wrong approach, but I want you to know you can talk to me.'

I hugged my duvet around me, wondering what I'd done to prompt her concern. Okay, so I'd had a couple of late-night crying fits in the upstairs bathroom. And maybe I'd been a little red-eyed after my afternoon in the lock-up, but these wobbles hardly constituted a reason to worry.

I nodded and pressed her hand, wanting this to be over. She seemed as embarrassed as I was, fiddling with the floppy collar of her flowery blouse. I knew she needed something to prove her approach had been worthwhile, so I said: 'That's really good of you, Sylvia, but what made you think something's wrong?'

She laughed, a sad chuckle. 'I don't think you realise how much we're alike, Sarah. I see you giving out exactly the same stress signals as I do.'

'Thanks, Sylvia, I'm sorry I'm so hard.'

She stroked her fingers through my hair. 'You're not hard,' she told me. 'You're an angel.'

I smiled at her and she left the room. I looked down at the envelope on my duvet. The problem with letters is that you've got no control over what the sender tells you. All I want from Mum is information about Melissa and Charlie, but she can't write about them without mentioning Lesley, and just seeing her name makes me feel sick.

I pick up the letter and give it an experimental squeeze.

At least five pages. Its plumpness reassured me, and I felt safe dropping it into my secret drawer. My mum only goes on when there's nothing to say. The day a thin letter arrives I'll open it immediately, certain to find *Sarah, Melissa's gone* inside.

Another aimless Saturday. I really ought to buy a stereo. It's stupid to let my mood be dictated by a DJ's whim. But I don't have time to get attached to records, and I'm sure they'd laugh at me if I went in to buy the songs from my teenage years, like Heaven 17 and the Fun Boy Three.

I'd intended to get out of tonight, but Mary'd pulled a sickie on Friday, and I couldn't be bothered to trek across to her flat. I'd told her to meet me by the Grand Central Hotel, hoping that if I followed the same route as last week I might be able to recapture some of that evening's magic.

I'd decided to ignore the decor of The Princess and dress up anyway, wanting every man's eyes to slide past Mary's cutie-girl affectation to the real woman beside her. As I laid out my clothes on the bed, I pictured a man watching me dress, imagining him shivering with anticipation as I picked out all the items he liked best.

Clichés seemed okay today. New stockings, a black mini. Usually I resisted Weston, but tonight I'd be happy to be mistaken for a local girl. I'd cut off any conversation about what we were missing in London, and respond to Mary's comments about Weston men as if they were unironic. It didn't matter if she thought I was an idiot, as long as she acknowledged the town was mine. As soon as I felt certain about my outfit, I stripped out of the blue jeans and purple T-shirt I'd slobbed about in all day, wrapped myself in a stiff towel, and walked to the bathroom to give my hair the hot-oil treatment.

When I returned from university, I thought Melissa would need twenty-four-hour attention and looked forward to giving myself up to this task. It would be a chance to atone for taking her for granted, a way of feeling good about myself again. (And, less nobly, it meant I wouldn't have to start looking for a job.) Melissa had never had many friends, and it'd feel good to have my shadow back. We'd be the Patton Spinster Sisters, getting over rejection through private jokes and picking on each other.

But on my first night back, I discovered that my sister already had a nurse. His name was Charlie, and he worked with her at Burger King. Mum said she felt certain nothing romantic was going on between them, and he was helping Melissa regain a sense of perspective about men. He'd been sleeping in my bedroom while I was away, but now he'd move into the lounge.

'Doesn't he have a home of his own?' I asked Mum.

'Don't be difficult,' she reprimanded, 'he saved your sister's life.'

Last week no one approached us. Maybe because three girls are more intimidating than two. More likely because last week we gave no indication we needed men. Tonight Mary and I were so busy scoping that our conversation never developed beyond the most rudimentary exchanges. I didn't even risk going to the toilet in case a stranger took advantage of my absence to approach Mary.

I know it's pathetic but I really wanted to be picked out first, especially after Mary had outwitted me with her clothes. Although she wore club outfits to work every single day, now we were actually inside a club she'd decided to dress down, choosing a dirty blue v-neck and baggy jeans. She was still wearing her PVC trainers, of course, but the overall effect made me look desperate.

'Dance?' she suggested.

I nodded and followed her across to the dancefloor. She rested her drink on a speaker and pulled her tobacco from her handbag. Her routine forced me to start dancing first. I closed my eyes and attempted a subtle variation on Vanessa's dance last week. When I opened my eyes, Mary was mimicking me, enlarging my gestures to make me look stupid. I dropped back into my normal dance, a subtle hips twist that was boring but hard to ridicule. Mary pretended her movements had nothing to do with me, changing from a straight copy by holding her arms level in front of her and clamping her lips on her roll-up.

A machine spat a dribble of dry ice at my feet. Mary mouthed along to the music. I looked round the rest of the club, checking if anyone was watching us. A man stood with his hands on the metal rail that ran round the edge of the dancefloor. I held his gaze. His reddish face and sharp cheekbones were made less imposing by his curly blond hair. He was wearing a pair of plastic trousers with metal poppers and a brown jumper without a shirt. Odd choice for a club in summer. Mary noticed me looking and moved round, creating space for him to join us. He danced across, holding his pint by the rim.

'So how do you two know each other?' Ben asked Mary.

She laughed. 'Sarah's my boss.'

'She doesn't look old enough. I had you two down as students.'

'I'm twenty-seven,' I said, offended.

'Don't worry,' he told me, 'I'm almost forty.'

'What d'you do?' Mary asked.

'I'm in plastics.'

'Which company?'

'P.L. Why, d'you know it?'

I nodded. 'One of your divisions does menus for us.'

'Oh right, you in catering then?'

'Not really. Promotions.'

He sipped his pint. Mary grinned at me. I didn't feel up to competing with her over Ben, and if she wanted him I'd leave her to it. I felt happy to let her take over the conversation and didn't care about being ignored. Ben didn't seem like the talkative type anyway, and after a few minutes I almost forgot he was there.

The Princess closed at one. Mary started moaning about hunger pains and Ben suggested we go to his place for cheese on toast. He lived in a small terrace by the train station, anonymous except for the cement mixer in the front garden.

'So who's up for a go on the Playstation?' Ben asked.

'You've got a Playstation?' said Mary. 'I haven't had a game in ages.'

Ben showed Mary through to the lounge, then took me to the kitchen. He had a caterer's toaster, a large metal contraption with a conveyor belt grill. I leaned against the counter and watched him feed it white bread.

'That looks expensive.'

'The toaster? I picked it up for a tenner. All of this stuff's from defunct hotels.'

'I like the table.'

'Genuine Formica top,' he said. 'Indestructible. Will Mary want butter?'

'I'd better ask. If you get it wrong she's bound to be furious.'

He laughed, and I left the kitchen.

Ben brought in the sandwiches on a thick plastic tray.

Mary had already loaded up the Playstation, and was now directing a three-inch bandicoot through a digital jungle. She was clearly an expert and her skill made the game look like a continuous cartoon. I particularly liked the way the baddies were traditionally friendly creatures like butterflies and snails.

My toasted sandwich tasted delicious. Ben had kindly made me a glass of Ribena and the sweet liquid revived my tastebuds after too much beer. He took his own sandwich and sat in the corner. He didn't seem in a particular hurry to seduce me or Mary, and I wondered if he'd just brought us back because he didn't like being alone.

I finished my sandwich and lay back on the settee. I kept watching Mary until she completed the game. As the bandicoot began his victory dance, Ben sat up in his chair.

'I've never seen anyone complete a game before.'

Mary grinned. 'I can do most of them. Once you've figured out one, the rest are pretty easy.'

'What about you, Sarah. Are you as good as Mary?'

'I've never played.'

'Do you want to have a go then?'

'No thanks. Can I use your toilet?'

'Of course. It's at the top of the stairs.'

I pulled the flush and switched off the bathroom light. Mary was waiting for me on the landing. She'd taken out her hairgrip and her damp hair hung down into her eyes.

'I told Ben we'd share a bed if that's okay. It'll make us seem more mysterious.'

She walked past me and left the bathroom door open while she washed her face. Ben came up to move a double mattress into the spare room.

'I've only got the one mattress,' he said. 'I hope that's okay.'

'We'll be fine,' Mary assured him, 'see you for breakfast.'

Mary fell backwards as she sat on the mattress, using her hands to steady herself.

'My feet really stink,' she said, 'it's these trainers.'

'I'm used to it,' I told her. 'Working in the alley.'

She put her shoes outside the door and examined her feet. 'These children's plasters are useless,' she said, poking her fingers beneath the sticky pad, 'they're making my blisters worse.'

Mary pulled her v-neck over her head and unbuttoned her jeans. Her stomach was paler than mine and she had a blue bow at the front of her knickers.

'I can't be bothered to undress,' I said, flopping down on the mattress. Mary switched off the light and lay down beside me. She put her arm around my stomach. I flinched.

'It's okay,' she told me, 'I only want to spoon you.'

I didn't reply, flustered by the feeling of her body against mine. Her breath smelt of Kronenbourg and Clorets. I wriggled free.

'Sorry,' I said, 'it's nothing personal. I just get a bit claustrophobic.'

I moved to the far right of the mattress, pulling my legs out of reach. Mary waited a moment, then asked: 'Can I just rest my feet against you then? I sleep so much easier if I know someone else's in the bed with me.'

'Okay.'

I felt her warm pads press against the backs of my thighs. I waited until I was certain she was asleep, then pushed them away.

5

Sunday

Henry loves church. He pays no attention to the sermons and likes to rub his leg against mine when the vicar is speaking, but no one could question his commitment to worshipping God. Every Sunday at seven I have to come over to dress with him, and he's always got fresh flowers for our buttonholes.

I managed to unstick myself from Mary without waking her, and felt happy and healthy inhaling the seabreeze on my way to Brighter Futures, Henry's rest home. He was lying awake on his white linen sheets, the Sunday shirt I'd bought him unbuttoned down past the crescent of his vest. He stood up to embrace me, then sniffed my hair.

'You went out last night?'

'Yes.'

'With Paul?'

'With Mary.'

'Who's Mary?'

'A friend.'

He smiled. 'You never talk about your friends. Do you think I'll steal them?'

'They're not your type.'

Henry took my hands. 'You look lovely.'

He hadn't shaved, and his white bristles and rolled-up sleeves reminded me why I fancied him. His earnest compliment made me feel guilty and I wanted to tell Henry I hadn't dressed this way for him.

I watched his eyes as he stroked his fingers down the back of my legs, feeling him rubbing the heel of his hand twice over the bump of my suspenders. I could see he was excited, and felt hopeful that he might finally be ready to make love to me again.

He released me and walked to the sink. I watched him lather the soap. When Henry's wife died he spent five years taking luxury cruises, and once told me that he treats his room as he did his cabin. He uses the wardrobe, the bed and the sink. When he leaves he'll pack a suitcase and throw away his paperback thrillers. The only sign anyone's living here is the tray of food on the floor.

'Don't you want your breakfast?' I asked.

'Why? Are you hungry?'

'Only if you don't want it.'

'No, go on, help yourself.'

I picked up the tray and rested it on my lap. I quickly gulped down the grapefruit and bran flakes, wanting to replace the stale taste that stayed with me from the night before.

As soon as I finished, I licked my fingers and rubbed them across the translucent hair-oil stain on Henry's pillow. Holding my fingers beneath my nose, I tried to isolate this specific ingredient of his scent. When I was a teenager, I used to spray whole cans of my first boyfriend's deodorant under my sheets and inhale as if it was drugged air that would transport me back to him.

'It's okay,' Henry said, 'they change the cases on Mondays.'

I like church too, and although it's played a destructive role in my relationships, I've always suspected that one day I'll undergo a full conversion. My parents aren't Christians, so God's house has always seemed a safe place to shelter. I've spent hours sitting alone in cathedrals and church museums, wondering what a good person would come here to think about.

Henry expects nothing of me. He's happy if I ignore everything from the greetings before to the farewells afterwards, as long as my bottom's next to his on the pew. And there's little danger I will be disturbed by the service, as the congregation knows the vicar's having an affair with a woman from the choir, and he's bought our silence by providing sermons that make us feel good rather than guilty.

Henry steered me into an empty pew at the back of the church. Instead of leg rubbing, today his hand quickly slipped under my skirt. He began by stroking my stocking tops, then started making patterns on the bare skin of my leg. We rose for the opening hymn and first few prayers, then as we sat back down the patterns turned into letters, his secret message confirming the return of his lust.

'Let's skip lunch today,' he said, and we took the quickest route from the church to Brighter Futures. I looked at the Old Pier on the way back, trying to shape it into my dream of The Pleasure Palace. The ramps would have to go, of course, and the whole thing had to be widened. But Henry was pulling me along, and I had no time to complete my vision.

He locked his door, closed the curtains and stripped the bed. 'You really do look beautiful, Sarah,' he said, lying back against the bare mattress.

I climbed on top of him, thinking he'd want to undress me. I felt a little anxious, worried about the amount of time that had elapsed since we last had sex. I hate it when too much emphasis is placed on a single event, especially a fuck.

'Come on, Henry, say something.'

His white hair was curling against the pillow and I leaned down to kiss his dry, open mouth, pushing my breasts against his chest.

'What is it, Henry?' I asked. 'What do you want to do?'

'Everything.'

I stared at the opal sheen of his freshly shaven chin. Looking at his supine body beneath mine, I wondered how he expected me to react to his submissiveness. Before now, Henry'd always taken charge, undressing me and turning my face away. He's got a thing about my bum and says he needs it constantly in view if he's going to come. Desperate to startle Henry into action, I climbed down from the bed and walked to the centre of the room, unfastening my stockings with my back towards him, then rolling my skirt and underwear down over my thighs so he'd get glimpses of my arse but the meat of me'd remain hidden by my blouse. I felt certain that seeing the silk struggle to keep me decent would draw him across, but when I looked over my shoulder he remained rigid on the bed, clenching his fists as if willing himself to remain unmoved by my display.

All I wanted to do was end this moment. If he couldn't express his desires, I'd guess them myself and rush through them. I turned round and unbuttoned my blouse midway and pulled back the material so he could see my breasts. I hoped that once he saw my inverted nipples and pimply neck, he'd stop looking at me with such awe. I dragged myself across to the bed, deliberately keeping my eyes away from him and trying to emphasise my willingness to do anything. Unlacing his shoe, I pulled off his worn sock and put his foot on my thigh. I did the same thing with his other shoe and then pulled down his light blue trousers.

His muscles felt so tight as I kissed the inside of his legs and stroked my tongue up towards his underwear. I kept expecting him to stroke my hair, or groan, or do anything normal. But his only movement was a quick shudder as my tongue dwelled on his calves. At first I thought this was a good sign, but then I saw the gluey blob oozing through the blue cotton of his supermarket briefs.

I didn't know what to do so I kept kissing, hoping that if I went on long enough he'd get aroused again and I could pretend I hadn't noticed his little accident. Then I felt his hands fold round my head and grip my jaw, as if I was a dog that had to be restrained.

'It's ruined, isn't it?' he said.

'Come on, Henry, we just went too quickly, that's all,' I said. 'It was new and strange. If you change everything in one go no wonder it doesn't work. Besides, it has been a while.'

He stared at me. I kissed his chest. 'It really isn't a big deal. Why are you taking it so seriously?'

'Because you'll never do it again.'

'Don't be stupid. We can try again next week. I'll come round on Thursday and we'll have an afternoon in bed instead of going to a restaurant.'

'But your clothes.'

'I'll wear them again.'

'It won't be the same.'

'I wasn't going to tell you this,' I said, 'and don't be offended, but I didn't wear these clothes for you. I put them on last night to go out and I ended up sleeping at a friend's house.'

'I thought you said you went out with Mary.'

'I did.'

'So it was her house you stayed at.'

'Yes.'

'Then why did you say a friend's house instead of Mary's house? You'd already told me her name.'

'I don't know. It's just a habit of mine. I can't stand people who expect you to remember the names of all their friends just to keep up with the stories they tell you.'

'Next time say the same. If you stayed at Mary's house, say Mary's house, don't say a friend.'

'Okay. I'm sorry.'

'Because either it's a lie and you didn't stay at Mary's, or it's true and it sounds like you're trying to make a mystery out of it to upset me.'

He went to the sink to wash himself. I felt annoyed that he was turning away from me, but tried to keep my voice even.

'Let's go for a drink,' I suggested.

'I don't want to go out,' he replied.

'Then let's get a bottle and stay in. You said you hadn't done that for a while.'

He stopped soaping his thigh. 'Would you stay here tonight?'

'Of course,' I said, 'if that's what you want.'

'What I want is for the cleaner to come in tomorrow and find you sitting on top of me and going at it so fast we don't even notice her.'

I laughed. 'It's not me you want at all, is it? You want some scandal.'

He pulled up his trousers and turned around. It was the first time I'd seen him like this, and I wasn't sure if I felt affection or anger. He was too tall and broad to look fragile, but there was anxiety in his expression, as if I'd challenged him to a fight instead of tried to have sex with him. He walked back to the bed and told me to turn around.

'Oh, Sarah,' he said, holding up my hair and kissing the nape of my neck.

I looked down at my toes, remembering how sexy I'd felt when I painted varnish on them the previous night. Where my big toenail is supposed to meet the skin, there's a tiny gap that sometimes aches. I have a recurring nightmare where I pull the skin away from the nail and the whole of my toe peels away from the bone like pink plasticine. Last night I'd brushed the varnish right up to the skin and it'd felt as if I was sticking myself back together, saving myself from the possibility of pain.

Over the rest of the day, Henry's mood worsened. We drank a bottle of Southern Comfort together, refilling our glasses with a drunk's resolution. Even when neither of us wanted any more, the bottle had to be finished.

'What's Paul like in bed?' he asked.

'Come on, Henry, I'm not going to get into this.'

'That good?'

'It's not fair to ask me a question like that. I don't ask you about your wife or your old girlfriends.'

'Do you want to know about my wife?'

'Henry, please. This isn't like you.'

But my protests didn't stop him. Something had changed in his mind, and with every extra drink he became more convinced that I'd deliberately tried to embarrass him. By nine o'clock we were both exhausted and I undressed for bed, trying not to feel anxious about sleeping here.

Neither of us could get to sleep so early and I could feel Henry trying to get hard again by rubbing himself against me. Eventually he said: 'I think you'd better go.'

'Why?'

'I don't find you attractive any more.'

'What?' I demanded, so shocked and upset that I instinctively pulled the sheet away from him.

He started crying. 'I didn't mean that.'

I got out of bed and reached for my skirt. 'I don't care, Henry, I'm going home.'

'No,' he said, 'please, I'm sorry, I really am. I've drunk too much and I'm ashamed because I can't satisfy you.'

He was really sobbing now, genuine gasps that made the muscles in his back move in a sweet, vulnerable way. I sat down on the mattress and lifted his head onto my legs.

'You really don't understand, do you, you stupid old man. I don't care if you make love to me or not. The thing I liked about us . . .'

'Liked?'

'Like. The thing I like about us is the relaxed way we do things. If you're hard, we might as well take advantage of it. If not, well, that's never stopped us before.'

'Thank you, Sarah,' he said, 'thank you for everything.'

I lay down beside Henry and put my arms around him. I was too weary to think about what he'd said, or whether I really did forgive him, and just wanted to get to sleep before we had another row.

Some time during the night I felt two hands bundle me up and return my body to the empty side of the mattress. A familiar sensation. Not just Henry's hands, but those of other lovers too. All my lovers. Almost all. The man I marry will be happy to hold me all night, waking me with his morning erection pressed into my back.

5

Tuesday

Paul handed me a spotlight.

'Take this out to the car and put it in the boot.' He threw me his keys. 'Be careful. The bulb's fragile.'

I nodded and leaned to one side, adjusting my fingers around the black metal handle. Then I tottered back through the office with the box up against my thigh, trying to stop the screws tearing my tights.

Paul'd parked in his usual space by the town hall. I folded a petrol-soaked blanket around the light, tucking it against the inner wall of the boot. I let myself into the car and turned on the stereo, hoping for a few minutes to check through the glove compartment.

My sister insisted on having Charlie with her at all times. Any chance of having a proper conversation was impossible with his constant presence in the corner of her room. The only way I could get any information about Melissa's breakdown was through Mum, and she was hardly the most reliable source.

Mum told me Melissa had developed an obsessive crush on a boy from her sixth form college. She'd known about it but hadn't considered the relationship serious, and saw no reason why Melissa's feelings wouldn't be reciprocated. After all, she said to me, the two of you are kind and attractive young women. Why wouldn't any boy be interested?

But Melissa had managed to find someone who genuinely didn't like her, and her attempts to win his affections only increased his distaste. Mum advised her to snub him for a few days, hoping this might bring him round. He remained uninterested, telling his friends how relieved he felt now she'd stopped chasing him. Two days later, Melissa resumed her campaign.

Charlie was the one who took her to the hospital. She'd been missing for twenty minutes during a busy shift at Burger King, and he found her in the employee toilets. Shaking, incapable of speech, she'd taken to her breasts with a tiny penknife that used to belong to our dad. When Mum arrived, the doctor told her Melissa was suffering from clinical depression.

'I'm ready today,' I told Paul.

'What for?'

'Talking.'

'What about?'

'Whatever. You. Your wife.'

'I don't need to talk. Things are sorted now.'

'It doesn't have to be bad things. You can tell me how happy you and Iona are if you like.'

'Why?'

'It'll be nice.'

'Why?'

'Because last time you tried to talk to me I felt insecure

and couldn't give you the support you needed. Things are different now.'

'Why?'

'You know why. Because we're going to persuade people to give us money to fulfil your dream. A dream that includes me.'

Paul looked at me. 'You're different today.'

'I'm happy, that's all. Let's talk about your wife.'

'I don't know if I can, just like that.'

'You wanted to talk before.'

'Yeah, and I did talk.'

'I know you did. But I wasn't very receptive.'

'I don't mean to you. I talked to someone else.'

I looked at him. 'Who?'

'Mary.'

'I see.'

Paul leaned forward. 'Don't get angry. It wasn't a big thing. We were just chatting and it came out naturally.'

'Let's just have a chat then. Who's coming tonight?'

'No one you know, apart from that woman from Clevedon. Business people.'

'Are you happy with me?'

'Of course. Why?'

'We haven't seen much of each other lately. I thought you might be going off me.'

'Is this because I talked to Mary?'

'I'm surprised you told her about Iona, that's all.'

'It's not like I kept it from you. You were the one who didn't want to talk about it.'

'Well, I want to talk about it now.'

'I told you, I don't know if I can.'

'Try.'

He sighed. 'Look, Sarah, I really can't talk to you about this. It's just something you can't understand.'

I gave up and sat back, amazed at how frustrated I felt. I

knew Paul was getting annoyed, and didn't want to push him further. The sensible approach was to smile and forget it, but it felt hard to ignore my feelings today.

'You are okay, aren't you?' he asked.

I swallowed. 'I'm fine.'

'It's really not a big deal, Sarah. Just leave it.'

'Okay.'

'Let's just have some peace now, okay?'

'No problem.'

We had to walk across the rocks to get to the Old Pier.

'I've arranged for one of the local fishermen to bring the investors across in a rowboat. I thought it would add to the intrigue.'

I smiled and tried to fit my foot safely onto the next rock. It'd been mild for a week now, and it felt good to be outside. We reached the last rock and scaled the shortest of the black struts. Paul tried to unlock the red metal doors, but his key wouldn't turn. He looked at me and melodramatically removed a can of WD-40 from his suit pocket. He squirted the lock, twisted the handle and pushed the doors open. When I looked inside, I understood why we'd started our preparation so early.

Paul picked up the item nearest to him. The life jacket's rotten lining split and dropped its innards onto the floor. Everything was covered in a layer of flaky black dust that looked like burnt paper. There was a strong smell of contained decay, like those school experiments where you leave an apple to rot under a glass beaker. It looked like the garage had been used for storage after it was abandoned by the RNLI and there was a row of glass cases along the back wall. Paul and I looked at each other and immediately headed over to uncover them.

Beneath the tarpaulin we found six machines from an

old penny arcade, including a strongman punch bag and a gypsy fortune teller. Paul, of course, couldn't resist, taking his coat off and handing it to me as he hammered his fist into the leather ball.

The jolt to the mechanism caused something inside to release and the old machine spat tuppenny pieces onto the dirty floor. Paul rescued one from the dust and slipped it into the sixth machine, which looked like a pair of binoculars on a metal stand.

'You'll like this, Sarah.'

I took his position at the machine. A black and white woman was dancing in front of a grey curtain, shedding an item of clothing with each jerky movement. I stared at her face but it was hard to identify her features. She could be any stranger from the past, the strip of film as meaningless to me as another person's school photograph. I stood back and Paul took my place. He remained there until the machine clicked.

'They always cut out just before the good bit,' he said, taking another tuppence from the floor. 'It's a pity you're not going to do an act like this tonight.'

I ignored him, wondering why he was so eager to belittle me today. Moving across to the fortune teller, I took a tuppenny piece and set her off. Her angular face lit up and her moles glowed as she selected a card, swinging across and dropping it down into the tray by my knees:

BEWARE THE FAMILIAR – IT MAY NOT BE AS
SAFE AS YOU THINK.

'Hah,' I said, 'look at this, Paul.'

He took the card. 'What does it mean?'

'It means I should dump you and look for someone who'll be nice to me.'

'Oh, come on, Sarah, don't make a fuss. We're going

to have a great night, so stop being moody and let's get on.'

It took us until five to clear the floor. We decided to incorporate some of the more interesting debris into the design of our spaceship. We put the fortune teller and the punch bag on either side of the stage area, then we dusted off the remains of a lifeboat to turn it into seats.

Once the garage was clean we ate the packed dinner Sylvia had made us. There was still work to be done before the investors arrived at seven, but the second half of our preparation was more relaxed. I felt comfortable with Paul now, forgetting my earlier irritation.

He looked great in his dinner jacket, and I interrupted him to kiss his legs and rub his balls through his underwear before he pulled up his trousers. He sat back on the lifeboat as I unzipped my flimsy work skirt and removed my blouse.

'You have such an excellent body,' he told me. 'Why are you embarrassed about it?'

'I'm not embarrassed.'

'Don't be stupid, Sarah. I know you're embarrassed. I do have a wife, remember?'

'What's that got to do with it?'

'My wife is the biggest tease imaginable. She sleeps in a nightdress and when we haven't had sex for a while she has this trick with her underwear. In the morning, she goes over to her underwear drawer, chooses a pair of knickers that she knows I like and then pulls them up under her nightdress. Then, as she's talking to me, she walks over to the bed and takes off her nightdress. She knows exactly where I'm staring. So she puts her fingertips under the elastic and adjusts her knickers, giving me a second's glimpse of what I can't have.'

'I don't understand how that relates to me.'

'The point is that anyone who can tease somebody like that knows the power of her beauty. She must look incredible, or suffer from serious delusions. And yet my wife, who can drive me into a frenzy, thinks she's ugly. All women are embarrassed about their body, it's just in your case it stops you having fun.'

I ignored him and took my dress from the purple Liberty bag it was wrapped in. The dress was made out of pale blue PVC with a low neckline and long sleeves. It was incredibly revealing, but it was so nice that I didn't worry. It felt more like having a second skin than being naked, and the PVC hugged every part of my body.

Paul stood up and walked outside. I could tell he was pissed off, but didn't think I'd done anything wrong. I seemed like such a magnet for emotion at the moment. Men are so temperamental. I felt like doing something cleansing, but the only think I could think of was a cigarette. And in spite of my lapses I was still trying to quit, so I'd stopped carrying them. I was forced to go and ask Paul for one. I expected him to tease me about breaking my vow, but he handed me his packet without saying anything. I kissed him, and put my hand on his shoulder. He stared at me, and I felt scared. Then I looked at my watch and asked him if it was okay if I went for a walk before the show.

When I walked out on stage, the lights were too bright for me to see the investors, but I could hear Paul's voice, complimenting me as if I was competing for the long-forgotten honour of being Miss Weston. I stared straight into the bulbs, dazzling myself and setting off scarlet buzzes behind my eyes. I'd matched my dress with plastic hairgrips and cheap jewellery, trying to emphasise an availability that would stop them feeling scared by me. I grinned out into the darkness and pushed up my gelled hair. When I closed my eyes I could picture Paul's club so clearly, only in my imagination it was a genuine spaceship and not a tacky imitation. Listening to the waves outside, I imagined they were the motors of the ship and I concentrated so intensely that I could feel the whole pier lifting up, sucking the struts back into the body of the ship and heading into space, taking me to a safety far beyond the stars.

5

Thursday

Henry made me sit on a bench while he went to get the clubs and balls. I felt embarrassed and overdressed. I'd worried all week about what to wear today. At first I thought Henry'd feel betrayed if I didn't dress exactly as I had last Sunday. But since then I'd decided that perhaps it'd be best not to remind him of his failure. So now I was about to play Crazy Golf wearing black boots with a square toe and a high heel, sheer grey tights, and short brown dress under a cream top. It wouldn't seem important if Henry was being nice to me, but he'd hardly looked at me since picking me up from opposite the solarium, and his decision to spend the afternoon putting balls across purple tarmac seemed a deliberate taunt.

He returned with the clubs and handed one to me. The plastic grip had worn smooth and the head was chipped.

'How do you want to do this?' he asked. 'Shall we have a par, or just count how many shots we take?'

'I don't mind.'

'It seems a bit pretentious to have a par, doesn't it? Let's just stick to counting shots.'

I placed my ball on the starting mat. The first hole was a straightforward putt, and I finished it in two strokes.

'How's Paul?' Henry asked, lining up his shot.

'Okay.'

Henry looked at me. He gets this strange look in his eyes when he's waiting for my permission to attack Paul. I didn't feel like granting it today and kept quiet. Henry nodded and returned to his shot, knocking the ball across the short distance to the hole.

'Well done,' I said.

'So I'm one in front,' he said, 'and I get to go first.'

There was a young couple with a small child playing the next hole, and we had to wait until they'd finished. In spite of the weather, the child was wrapped up in a red padded suit, making it hard to determine its sex. The black-patent shoes and white socks suggested a girl, but the parents' own strange clothes made any certain conclusion difficult. The child wasn't much larger than the kid's club she'd been given, and the only way she could play was to hold on to her father's hands as he hit the ball for her.

The couple ahead moved on to the third hole. Henry set up his shot and whacked the ball too hard. It bounced off the rusted metal barrier at the back of the hole and skipped up onto the pavement running down towards the road. Henry chased after it and nipped out between two cars to get it back. Trotting over, he tucked in his shirt and stood behind me.

'That's my lead gone,' he said. 'You have a go and then I'll start again.'

I lined up my shot, trying to look intent because I thought it'd be the best way to get Henry's attention.

'Good shot,' he said, as I sunk the ball.

'Henry,' I said, 'can we stop please?'

'Stop?'

'I don't think Crazy Golf is for me.'

'But you're doing brilliantly. Are you sure you don't want to finish the round?'

'Let's just go to The Wayfarer, okay?'

Henry smiled at me. I wanted to see the usual grace in his expression, but instead he looked triumphant, as if he'd taught me something. He took my club and returned to the hut. The couple ahead were looking at me, and I felt ashamed.

'What's wrong?' Henry asked when he returned. 'You look miserable.'

'I'm fine,' I told him. 'Just hungry, that's all.'

'You should have said something,' he said. 'Would you like an indigestion tablet?'

'No thanks. I'll be okay once I get some food inside me.'

Most nights Charlie sat with my sister until long after she'd fallen asleep. When Melissa first returned from the hospital, this was a necessary precaution, as she usually awoke with nightmares and he was the only one who could calm her down. But that hadn't happened for weeks now, and I thought there was definitely something creepy about the way he stayed with her while she slept. I'd watch them from the staircase, wondering what Charlie was thinking as he stared at her dormant body. Then one night after coming back late from the pub, I decided to confront him.

His face was furious as he pushed me from Melissa's bedroom, telling me we should leave her in peace if we wanted to speak. I followed him down to the lounge and demanded to know why he was so interested in my sister. He said he was simply being a good friend and I told him I didn't buy it. No one would be this kind without a reason. If he didn't fancy her, what was he doing here?

When he went silent, I immediately regretted pushing

him. The angry adolescent in me was determined to prove that there was no such thing as selfless generosity, but now he seemed about to admit his motivations, I wished I hadn't been so suspicious. I didn't really want to hear about Charlie's dark side.

The first thing he wanted to make clear was that he hadn't set out to be Melissa's saviour. But he'd always had religious tendencies and when he discovered my sister bleeding in the toilets, he couldn't help believing that the coincidence had been preordained. At the time, Charlie explained, he'd been suffering from terrible guilt about the way he'd treated women. Although he was currently celibate, he'd often been the object of obsession, and frequently demeaned the women who fell for him. He seemed to have a superhuman ability for driving women crazy, and until now had always exploited their extreme emotions.

He told me about all the women who'd threatened to kill themselves, and how awful he felt about the one who'd succeeded. He described how easy he found it to pick up women, and recounted a story about a girl at university who'd masturbated against the doorhandle of his locked room, using the comebreath to cry out *'I hate you'* while he and his new lover cowered inside. It should have sounded like ridiculous boasting, but looking at his cute, angular jaw in the dim light, it wasn't hard to understand how someone might be obsessed with him.

I listened as he explained how he liked being with Melissa because she genuinely wasn't interested. He could explain how oppressive it felt to be loved by someone you didn't like, and tell her everything he wanted to say to all those women who'd cried in his arms. It was a test of his ego, and a shot at redemption. In short, his reasons for helping my sister were exactly the same as mine.

Henry gave the waitress our order. Then he asked: 'Do you like working for Paul?'

'It's okay. It's not my dream job or anything.'

'I don't mean the job. Do you like the idea of working for Paul?'

'I don't understand.'

'The relationship. Is it more exciting because he pays your wages?'

I stared at him. He had an eyelash on his cheek. 'Why have you started worrying about Paul? I've hardly seen him lately.'

'I'm not asking about Paul. I'm asking about you.'

'We don't talk about the money,' I lied.

'How would you like it if Paul was in debt to you?'

'Why'd you ask?'

'If you agree, I'm going to give you the money Paul pays me every month. It's not a lot, but it's enough to live on. Or if you want, you can continue working, and put Paul's cash in the bank.'

'Why?'

'I don't need it.'

'That's no reason.'

'I'm lazy, Sarah. I've always been lazy. My mum used to say the only reason I was born ten days late was because it was too much trouble to leave her womb. She breast fed me until I was four. While all the other kids were learning to read and write, all I wanted to do was sit in a corner on my own. To this day, I've never learnt how to swim or ride a bike.'

He stared out of the window.

'I was lazy in school, and in my first few jobs. It was only because my parents were wealthy that I'm alive today. Then, when I was fifteen, I met my perfect woman. Miss Weston, remember, Julie Shaw. I told you what happened to her, but not what happened to me. The moment I

saw Julie put her arm around Christian, I stopped being lazy.

'There is a comfort in never making an effort, but it's a lonely comfort. What keeps you going is the knowledge that you're playing with only four cards showing. But when you see other people succeeding with their mediocre hands, you have to make a decision. If you turn over that final card you're certain of victory, but it also means you have nothing in reserve.

'I wanted Julie, but more than that I wanted to turn myself into the sort of person Julie'd like. I went to my father and asked him if I could borrow some money. He'd kept me afloat before then, but this was the first time I'd asked for anything substantial. I was certain he'd refuse, but instead he seemed pleased I'd asked for the money, especially when I said I needed it for an investment.

'When I moved into business, I found people trusted me. I was always straight with everyone, and that won their respect. Once I made a connection, I stuck with that person, happy to thrive alongside others. I only invested in Weston, wanting my money to improve the place where I lived.

'I started off with restaurants, then moved into arcades. I had a tiny interest in everything, spreading my money wide. And all the time I was concentrating on improving myself. Of course, by now I was one of Weston's most eligible bachelors, and I hadn't escaped the attention of the local girls' mothers. It was time to forget about Julie and look at the other opportunities that now surrounded me.

'I dated for about a year, courting each girl for three months before crying off. I enjoyed the process, especially getting to know a girl's family, but the charms of each soon grew tiresome, and it wasn't long before I moved on to the next. But I couldn't live like that for ever, and knew that before long I'd get a name for myself. Mothers would talk, and I'd be dismissed as a dud.

'So I married Debbie, who was easily the best I'd had so far. And, to my surprise, I never regretted it. I chose Debbie because she seemed honest and kind, but she turned out to have as many levels as any other woman. She had no dark secrets, but she had layer after layer of warm humanity, an unfathomable depth of feeling. She loved me in a beautiful, complex way, and although I never meant to, I'm sure I hurt her countless times without realising.

'But all through my marriage, as I'm sure Debbie knew, I had this ambition to satisfy someone else. It started off as Julie, but after she committed suicide, the urge remained. After Debbie's death, it became even more acute. I have succeeded, but for whom? My daughter doesn't want my money, my son would squander it. And, besides, I would get no satisfaction from pleasing my children.

'Every time I think seriously about it, the person I keep coming back to is you. Think of this money as a little gift to start you off. A small taste of what you'll get after I'm dead.'

I looked for the waitress, wondering why she was taking so long with our meals. Henry was leaning halfway across the table, his elbows pointing at me.

'I don't know if I can accept,' I told him.

'Why not?'

'It's too large a commitment.'

'Where's the commitment?' he asked. 'The money has no bearing on our relationship. Even if you told me you never wanted to see me again, I'd still want you to have it.'

The waitress finally appeared, and I made a fuss about sauces and cutlery to give me a moment to think. I felt so angry at Henry. I'd worried all week about how to restore the balance between us, and had been prepared to do anything to emphasise how important our relationship was to me.

'So what do you say?' he asked.

'I don't know yet.'

'That's fair enough.'

He started picking at his meal. I thought it was my refusal to give him an immediate answer that was troubling him, but then he said: 'I've got something else I want to say to you, but I don't want you to associate it with the offer I've just made.'

'Okay.'

'I don't want you to come round on Sundays any more.'

'I see.'

'I know it's not the best attitude, and that it would be more sensible to get straight back on the horse that threw me off, so to speak, but I don't want to think about my problem for a while. It's not a permanent thing and eventually I'd like us to sort it out together, but I need a little break to get my confidence back.'

'What about Thursdays?'

'Thursdays will carry on the same as usual.' He reached for my hand. 'This isn't my way of stopping us. I'm trying to make us stronger than ever. In the meantime, we're going through some temporary changes, that's all.'

He patted my hand and looked down at his dinner. His fringe fell over his left eye. My tongue checked the small ulcer in the pocket of my cheek, then moved on to a string of trapped beef fat. I looked at the clock behind the counter. Almost two.

Another hour and I'd be free to go.

5

Saturday

The moment I saw Mary I wanted to slap her. She was my lover's new confidante, hearing all the problems he couldn't bring himself to share with me. All week at work I'd managed not to think about their relationship, telling myself that I was the one with Paul by my side. But now we were about to go out together, I wanted to drag her to the ground and demand she detailed every conversation she'd ever had with my boss.

She was wearing a purple asymmetric top which showed off her shoulders and went well with her gelled hair. She asked me how I was. I told her I felt fine.

'What's wrong?' she asked.

'Nothing.'

'I'm not late, am I?'

'No, you're not late.'

We started walking to The Black Baron, an old man's pub where we'd agreed to meet Ben. It wasn't really my scene, but now Mary had arranged it, I didn't want to let Ben down.

'Sarah, d'you mind if we slow down a bit? It's hard to keep up in these trousers.'

I slowed down. She put her hand on my shoulder,

catching her breath. We walked like that until the end of the street when Mary demanded, 'Sarah, please, tell me what's wrong.'

I looked at her. 'Have you slept with Paul?'

'What?' she said, looking genuinely upset. 'Why would you think that?'

'I just want to know.'

Mary exhaled. 'No, of course not.'

'He said you'd been having conversations.'

'About sleeping together?'

'About his marital problems.'

'Not for ages. And they weren't flirtatious conversations. Did he say he was interested in me?'

'He said you're a good listener.'

'Sarah, don't take this the wrong way, but after talking to Paul he's the last person I'd want to sleep with.'

I nodded. She sounded convincing, and I could easily understand how listening to Paul's problems would stop someone wanting him. I felt embarrassed at my jealousy, and forced myself to put my arms around her.

'I'm sorry,' I said, 'I should have trusted you.'

She smiled. 'It's okay.'

I knew I had to tread carefully if I wanted Charlie. The most important thing was to run it by Melissa, which was impossible when he was always with her. But I told my sister I wanted a private chat and she managed to persuade him to go to the cinema.

'Are you sure it's okay?' I asked her. 'I don't want to tread on your toes.'

'Charlie?' she said. 'I admit I thought about it. But he was the one who rescued me and I know if I sleep with him, I'll get obsessed again. And I don't want to end up thinking of love as an illness.'

I looked at my sister and felt terrified that she'd gained so much wisdom from so little experience. Then, for the last time I can remember, I held Melissa and told her I loved her.

Ben was already waiting at The Black Baron. He sat at a table with a group of people who's names he quickly recited and I immediately forgot. They were just the kind of people I expected him to be friends with, cheerful thirtysomethings who still believed that being in Weston was a brilliant laugh. Most of them were only down for the weekend, safe in the knowledge that any chaos they caused here could be forgotten by Monday morning. Mary made more of an effort than I did, taking the trouble to find out their jobs and interests.

I knew it was a mistake to come out tonight. On top of the embarrassment I felt about showing Mary just how neurotic I can get, I still hadn't recovered from Henry telling me he wanted to end our Sunday afternoons together. There was only one thing that could improve my mood, and that was the gold liquid in the glass in front of me.

Any worries that Melissa might feel jealous about Charlie proved completely unfounded. Once I'd told her I fancied him she became the perfect matchmaker, putting all her energies into pulling us together. Her best trick was convincing Charlie that going out with me would stop her worrying about him leaving when she got better. For the next few weeks I kept my distance, wanting to give the idea time to settle in his head. Then Melissa told me she'd arranged for the three of us to spend a weekend in the country.

We stayed in the pub until almost midnight. Ben had invited his friends back to his house, but before we went there, the weekend visitors wanted a trip to the beach. As we started walking, we soon fell into pairs.

Mary grinned at me. 'What d'you think of Ben?'

'I like him. Are you going to make a play?'

'Maybe. It's just that I always feel like such a slag after a one-night stand.'

I laughed.

'Sarah,' she said, 'about what you were saying earlier. You do know I'd never go near Paul.'

'Yeah. It's not your fault. Men like to make you jealous, don't they?'

'His wife sounds like such a bitch. What's her name?'

'Iona.'

'I can't stand women like her. My mum was like that with my father. Women like Iona go for ambitious men because they know they're bound to feel guilty. They draw them in, then freeze them out. It's sickening.'

'I know.'

Mary looked at me. 'What's your relationship with Paul like? If you don't mind me asking.'

'I don't think I give him what he wants.'

'It's bollocks, isn't it? The way other people see adultery. My mother would have you stoned. But I think you give more to Paul than any wife could.'

I smiled at her. 'What makes you say that?'

'I've had maybe three conversations with Paul, and that was difficult enough. I've never met a man who needs so much support.'

'He wasn't always like that.'

'Still. It must be difficult.'

I didn't reply. Mary took my arm. 'Don't take this the wrong way, but to begin with I was really scared of you.'

'I could tell,' I told her. 'Why?'

'You seemed so self-contained. I could see you didn't need anyone. You seemed so secure, so powerful, so . . .'

'Hard?'

'No, not hard. You were kind to me, and tried to make me feel at home.'

'Not that I did a good job. You looked terrified that time on the pier.'

She laughed. 'I wasn't scared of you. I was scared of meeting someone who knew more than me.'

'That's very flattering, but . . .'

'Seriously, Sarah. You don't know what allure intelligence holds for me. Even though I went to a good school, I was always streets ahead of everybody else. I don't think of myself as clever, and yet, until you I've never met anyone who's challenged me.'

'I'm not intelligent. I don't even have a degree.'

'Come on, Sarah, if further education meant anything to me, do you think I would have studied textiles?'

I laughed, and we walked on in silence. I felt glad I was hearing her kind compliments after a few drinks, knowing they'd mean much less to me sober. I wondered if she was waiting for me to respond. Then she said: 'You're my only friend here, Sarah. You do know that.'

She smiled at me, then laughed as I tripped over the kerb.

I knew better than to go after Charlie straight away. Newly redeemed men are the hardest to pull, and I could tell he wasn't yet convinced that sleeping with me would be a virtuous act. Melissa had warned me that he thought she was pushing us together as an exercise in self-destruction, and it took two days of playing happy families before he'd agree to spend more than a few moments alone with me.

By day three, I'd decided the only way to get through

to Charlie was a late-night attack. My body was the best argument I could offer him. After I was certain Melissa was asleep, I sneaked across to his tent, opened the flap and slipped inside. I knew he was awake, so I stretched my fingers over his mouth. He didn't move. I unbuttoned his lumberjack shirt and stroked my other hand up his vest, searching for his night-hardened nipples. I lay on my side, ignoring the prickle of the ground and pushing myself against him. I brushed my fingers down from his eyes and placed them between his lips. I checked his eyes. Still closed. His body felt much softer than I thought it would. His long hair and stubble had led me to expect that he'd be hairy all over, but his chest was surprisingly smooth. I still didn't know what I was going to do to him, but I knew I couldn't stop there. I stroked his chest until I could hear his breathing, then unbuckled his blue jeans. I pulled the buttons open and felt gratified by his hardness. He wasn't wearing any underwear and I smelt the unmistakable odour of soiled manhood. Cheese and fish, they say, but that's rubbish. Unwashed men smell of boiled potatoes. Unwashed women, lemon chicken. And I must be the only woman in the world who finds both smells a turn-on.

Charlie's balls were held down beneath his jeans, so I used my thumb to roll them out. He gasped as I stroked him, and as always happens when I'm with a new man, I couldn't stop myself pushing down further. I don't know if other people have similar markers, but I can't count a night as a conquest unless I've explored my lover's perineum. These muscles fascinate me, and if I was to make my own pornography, it would consist of thousands of shots of men trussed up with their legs open, and even though I'm profoundly heterosexual, I've often wondered if women's perineums would entice me as much as my own. I gripped Charlie there while I used my other hand to stroke the head of his cock, not stopping until I felt his spurt against my hand. Then he turned and looked at me. He was crying. In a love-constricted voice, he sobbed: 'Thank you.'

We'd reached the pathway down to the beach. The group was coming together again, private conversations giving way to a general chitchat. Ben made a joke about Mary and she poked her tongue out at him. Someone suggested skinny dipping and we all laughed in a hesitant way.

The others all sat around this one large rock, but I wanted some space on my own to think about Charlie. I walked towards the sea and then flopped onto the beach, unconcerned about my clothes. I rolled over in the sand and then pushed myself against the beach, squashing an impression of my body into the wet silica.

It didn't take Charlie long to escape my thoughts. I returned to considering Henry's offer. Not having a job would make things so complicated. My nine to five routine kept me sane, and I couldn't cope with filling seven empty days. Taking the money and sticking with March Entertainments seemed the most sensible option, especially as I could quit the bowling alley and have the nights to myself. But that seemed an admission that my crappy career meant something to me, a conclusion I felt desperate to avoid. And once I'd rejected these two routes, the only alternative was to refuse the money, and that seemed the biggest mistake of all. I decided to ask Henry for more time, hoping the answer would come to me.

I turned on my side to watch the others as they tried to build a fire. Ben seemed to have set his heart on Mary and stole her shoe to fill it with sand. Eventually they managed to get a little flame from an empty beer box and a few pieces of washed-up wood. They all went quiet for a minute, watching until it went out. Then Mary came over and sat next to me.

'Are you coming back?' she asked.

I nodded and stood up.

I could hardly walk straight as we returned to Ben's. One of his friends tried to talk to me, but gave up when I didn't respond. I was suffering from that horrible drunken lethargy when all you want is a space to lie out. Spreading myself out on the beach had made my body ready for sleep, and I could tell it resented this extra effort.

When we reached Ben's house, he immediately asked everyone what they wanted to eat. He was a good host, and he seemed happiest when taking care of his guests. I told him I didn't want anything and sneaked into the lounge, searching for a place to sleep. I took the chair in the far corner, knowing I could rest here without distracting the others from the Playstation.

Mary smiled at me.

I was back in the bedroom I'd slept in last week, although it didn't feel as comforting as before. It was light outside. Mary's face was pink and blotchy, but I was certain I looked worse.

'I hope you don't mind,' she said.

'Mind what?'

'I don't know why I'm so squeamish about sleeping with Ben. I'm sure they think we're lesbians.'

'How did I get here?'

'Ben and I carried you up. We tried to wake you but you kept smiling and shaking your head. Do you want some lunch?'

'What about breakfast?'

'Breakfast? It's after two. Ben's been a real sweetie and he's cooked us all Sunday lunch.'

I tried to wake myself up. My back felt as if I'd been beaten. Grit chafed my legs. I stood up and pulled back the duvet. The sheets were covered in mud and sand, with black streaks running along each fold. There were even shells and strips of seaweed caught up with the hair I had shed during the night.

'Don't worry,' Mary told me, 'he's a pretty relaxed guy.'

'Yeah, but still. Help me shake the worst of it out the window.'

We bundled up the sheet and slapped it against the outside wall.

'Sarah,' said Mary, 'what d'you think of Neil?'

'He's okay. Why?'

'Have you noticed he's got a crush on you?'

'What?'

'When he first came here he talked about you every day. Last week he didn't mention you once. That's a sure sign.'

We had a pleasant afternoon. Ben had made Sunday lunch the way I like it, with simple, separate parts. Chicken, carrots, boiled potatoes and peas, evenly spaced with no gravy. After lunch, I relieved myself of the guilt I felt about messing up Ben's bed by helping him clear up. At five o'clock, Mary and I wandered back home together, and I got her to tell me all about Neil's crush on me.

Friday

9th June

Dear Sarah,

I'm sad because you're not here with me. But this wouldn't matter if I knew you were doing something wonderful with your life. I know it's not a good idea to nag you at the start of this letter, but please read on. If I think you're not going to read this, I won't be able to continue writing. I've long since given up any hope of receiving a reply, but the fact that you've given me your address leads me to believe that you do, at least, want me to continue writing to you.

You were never really one for writing, so you probably have no idea how comforting it can be. But I want these letters to serve a purpose for you as well as me. I want to believe you're still interested in the lives of your family and friends. If I think you've given up on them, then I will too. But until then, passing news gives my social life a purpose, and I can feel happy knowing I am collecting anecdotes for you. I know you probably resent the fact that your mother is so intimate with your friends, but I love Charlie and Lesley, and as we've all been abandoned by you, our bond seems natural.

You were always cold and distant with your friends. Did you even like them? I always thought you confided in Lesley, but she thought you only shared your secrets with me. Personally, I'm not too sure you were intimate with anyone. I certainly haven't met anyone who claims to know you. What are you searching for, Sarah? Have you found it? Is that why you don't want to come back? What is there in Weston? How can those dreary seaside towns captivate you when there was nothing you liked in the whole of London?

I met your father last Wednesday. Now that so much time has passed, I find it easy to talk to him. I think that because our separation was so low-key, it took us both longer to get over it. If we'd fought before we broke up, there'd be no resentment, and no danger of reconciliation. There was a touching moment in my conversation with Pat when he went very quiet and then told me the reason he avoided me for so long after we separated was because he felt scared that if he saw me he wouldn't be able to go through with the divorce. When he said this, it made me think of you. Is there some reason why you don't want to see me? Are you scared that if you stay here you'll never have any independence? If so, I'm probably making it worse by becoming so close to your friends. If you want me to stop seeing them, just let me know. I'm only acting like this because you didn't leave any instructions before you went. I'm trying to do what you want me to do, but how can I know what that is if you don't tell me?

I've always believed you adore your father and sister, but as you have abandoned them also, maybe I'm wrong. I always felt excluded from you three after that year when your father put his back out and you were all home together all the time. I used to have to stop myself crying every time I came back from the day-care centre and found you all reciting the lines from some terrible children's TV programme. You had private jokes that went on for years, and although I knew you didn't mean it, I resented the implication that I was the outsider.

When I try to remember us being together as a family, I can only remember the occasions. I want to remember what it was like on ordinary days, but I can only recall the holidays in the caravan or your birthdays. And even then I can only see these times as how I wanted them to be, not how they really were. I can't remember which Christmases ended with laughter and which with smacks, only that I tried to prevent the latter. If by some miracle you do decide to answer this letter, could you describe a family moment you remember? It doesn't matter if it's horrible, or if you were pretending to be happy when you were really depressed. I just want to have some idea of what it was like for you.

I didn't tell you this before, but when you left I tore your room apart. I read your letters, your stories, your diary. I know it was wrong, but I was furious. I wanted to kill whoever it was who'd driven you away. I didn't care if it was me. In fact, I think I secretly hoped it was me. I wanted to find a list of every terrible thing I'd done, so I could change myself and you'd return. But all I found were dates and facts. How can you keep so much inside?

I know you probably hate the fact that I'm close to Charlie, but when you left he was the only one who understood how I felt. It sounds ridiculous, a forty-five-year-old woman asking a twenty-two-year-old to comfort her, but as soon as I saw his face I felt better. No one ever talks about the relationship between parents and their children's lovers, but I think one of the saddest times I can remember is those first few nights after you broke up with Charlie. I wanted you two to get married, and when Charlie stopped coming round I felt a greater sense of loss than when your father left.

Charlie and I have spent a lot of time talking recently. He's told me things I never knew about your relationship. He said you told him you didn't love him right at the start. He thought it was funny and a change from all the other girls who'd been devoted to him. He also thought you'd change your mind. He saw it as a challenge and believed that the day he made you beg for him would be the happiest of his life. Then he realised you would never love him and decided not to worry about it. He was happy with us, and it had been so long since he'd gone with someone else that he'd forgotten he could do it.

Then you both became friends with Lesley and he said that he saw a look in her eyes that he hadn't seen directed at him for years. He said he saw security in that look, and wanted to be safe again. He said that even though he never stopped loving you, or me, he needed his strength back.

The thing that amazed me most about his story was your absolute self-control. You never once told him you loved him, even when he was about to leave. You never begged him to change his mind, never referred to the relationship once it was over. And it's taken him three years to be able to talk about you.

I know all of this probably doesn't mean anything to you, but if it's possible for you to give some of your strength to someone else, you really should sort things out with Lesley. You may have a new life but the poor girl still feels guilty about everything. She thinks she's stolen your boyfriend, sister and mother, and that she was the one who forced you to leave.

Melissa still sleeps in your bed. She says she's trying to

preserve the dent you left in your mattress. I don't know if it's healthy or not, but I think she should be allowed to remember you however she wants. She also wears your clothes, but as you two always swapped outfits, I see no harm in that either.

She has a new boyfriend, her first since you left. His name is Joe and he seems reasonable enough, although I don't think you'd like him. He is good for her. He was transferred to Lloyd's and he's five years older than her. He seems sentimental, but then again Melissa feels safest with that sort of man. They seem to be happy and they're always playing with toys and puppets or reading to each other from children's books.

Please come back, if only to see your sister. She loves you so much, and cries because she thinks she's never going to see you again. I know that you want your own life, but you must understand that for years you were her closest friend and she has all these secrets she can't share with anyone else. I tell her to write to you, but she says she won't until she gets your permission.

I know that you're not nostalgic, and that I won't be able to persuade you to come back by reminding you of how things used to be, but if you did return, it could be any way you want. I always thought the strongest feature of our relationship was that we could change things, and I guarantee that we would all be prepared to shape our lives around you.

Love,
Mum

5

Wednesday

Paul called me into his office.

'How are you, Sarah?'

'Okay. Why?'

'I want to talk to you about our nightclub.'

I sat at his desk. 'Go on then.'

'What I want to ask you is, have your feelings changed since we did the presentation.'

'I don't understand.'

'Well, before we did the presentation you said you didn't like the idea of it becoming real too quickly. I wondered if you still feel like that.'

'Why?'

He opened his drawer and placed two A3 photocopies on the desk. Front covers of the *Advertiser* and the *Gazette*.

'Are these last week's?'

'Next.' He smiled. 'They've been sent to me for my approval.'

'I didn't know journalism worked like that.'

'It doesn't. For most people. But I'm responsible for ninety per cent of the advertising in these rags.'

I picked up the first photocopy. It was the larger of the two headlines, with a picture of Paul standing in front of the Old Pier. His grinning face took up the left-hand side of the photograph, with the pier stretching away behind him. LOCAL BUSINESSMAN IN PIER RENOVATION SCHEME. It was a surprisingly thorough article, describing Paul's ambition, his progress so far, and even detailing my performance in front of the investors. It ended by stating that this was just the kind of scheme needed to take Weston into the twenty-first century. I moved on to the *Gazette*. PLEASURE PALACE PIER PROJECT. The second article was slightly more sensational, emphasising the spaceship angle. It had a smaller photo of Paul and a reproduction of the plans.

'They've got your good side.'

He smiled. 'So you're okay about it?'

'Of course. I know you're doing it for us.'

'I am, Sarah. I am.'

It'd been hard to keep the dinner party from Paul. Every time I tried to arrange things with Mary he'd glide up behind us, eavesdropping. He's still not sure why I've got all these new female friends, and wants to check it's not a first step in escaping from him. I don't think he knows about Neil's attentions, but maybe I'm fooling myself and he'd be glad to pass me on.

We'd chosen Wednesday because it was a non-bowling night and I wanted to invite Amy and Vanessa. Mary lived across from the Odeon. Her flat was decorated just as I'd imagined, with taffeta wall-hangings and base-metal candlesticks. I made the salad while Mary prepared chicken in white-wine sauce. I put in lots of lettuce because I didn't know how many of our guests were vegetarians.

'Now,' I told Mary, 'the trick to a successful dinner party

is to have a few drinks beforehand. That way you're relaxed even before the guests arrive.'

There was half a bottle of wine left over from the sauce and Mary filled two tumblers, handing one to me as she relaxed against the kitchen cabinets.

'Have you seen Neil's place?' she asked.

'No. Is it like this?'

'Not really. He's sharing a maisonette with a couple who've run out of money. It's all open plan, so he doesn't get much privacy. The couple are weird, and Neil says he feels like their pet.'

We finished the bottle in the kitchen. Mary was more affected by the alcohol than I was, her cheeks beginning to redden and her voice becoming strident. We went into the lounge to check everything was ready for the party. I couldn't believe Mary was going to this much trouble for me. I knew she planned to seduce Ben tonight, but I was touched by her generosity.

Mary had made name cards for everyone at the party, each person arranged to help us achieve our respective aims. She took a fresh bottle from the table and unpeeled the seal.

We were halfway through the bottle when the first guest arrived. I wish I had Vanessa's body. Her body's so good that she can get away with anything. The nylon green dress she wore tonight was straight from New Look, but she still looked better than Mary and me.

'No Lee?' I asked.

'He's coming later.'

I stared at her. She held my gaze. It was impossible to tell whether this was true or an excuse. I felt proud Vanessa was my friend, and relished Mary's discomfort. She was staring at her legs and trainers and I knew she felt upstaged. I closed my eyes and imagined them fighting, wrapped tight together as they rolled across the floor.

I knew I ought to introduce Mary to Vanessa, but for the moment I was happy to let the silence continue. The most amusing thing was the way Vanessa kept her eyes down, occasionally glancing at me but refusing to acknowledge her host.

'What kind of music is everyone into?' she asked, looking at Vanessa. Vanessa shrugged. Mary turned to me. 'Sarah?'

'I don't mind.'

Mary opened the doors of her stereo cabinet and took out a handful of CDs. 'Bjork? The Fugees? A bit of acid jazz?'

'Fugees,' said Vanessa, her voice authoritative.

'Okay.' Mary opened the case and removed the silver disc. 'Any particular track?'

'Just put it on random.'

I didn't know the group but it sounded like the sort of thing they played on the radio. I felt peaceful sitting there listening to the stereo, and hoped the rest of the evening would be this pleasurable. I knew I'd taken a risk in alienating Mary. I didn't think she was that close to Neil, probably because Paul had succeeded in making them feel like brother and sister, but I sensed a connection there I didn't understand. Still, Mary needed my help to get Ben so maybe I was safe.

When I first met Lesley, she was wearing a pair of plain-glass Lennons, a grey pinafore and cream knee socks. I couldn't tell if her outfit was inspired by the chic schoolgirl fashion that had gripped Miss Selfridge and Chelsea Girl that year or a look she'd maintained since high school. I could smell her frustration from the moment I met her, an odour so strong I was surprised she wasn't tailed by dogs.

Lesley was Charlie's new project. Melissa had long since recovered and my boyfriend needed a new focus for his attentions. She was the daughter of a friend of his mother's, and had recently tried to poison herself. I tried to admire Charlie's altruism, but hated the way it'd become an accepted part of his personality. And as I watched Lesley take up smoking, pierce her ears and start dressing properly, it became harder and harder to feel sorry for her.

Amy arrived midway through the second song. She took off her clogs and sat between Vanessa's legs, talking to Mary as if she'd known her for ever. Mary seemed moved by Amy's attentions, and Vanessa allowed herself to be drawn into conversation, like a dogowner who will only accept someone after their pet has sniffed them out.

Ben arrived talking. 'That's a wonderful staircase you've got there,' he rushed, looking back through the open doorway.

Mary stared at him. 'What's wonderful about it?'

'The smooth curves and the brown glass. It's like something from a Seventies thriller.'

The others laughed at Ben's pretentious comment, but I could see what he meant. He seemed confused by their amusement, pressing his thumb into the flesh of his arm. Mary went to him, and brought him into the room.

'This is Ben,' she said. 'He's in plastics.'

Amy laughed. 'Sounds posh.'

'The girls work with me,' I told him, 'in entertainment.'

'For goodness' sake, Sarah,' said Vanessa, 'you make us sound like prostitutes.'

Amy looked at Ben. 'We work at the bowling alley.'

He nodded. The music continued in the background, filling the space. Ben turned a chair round from the table and sat facing us. I poured him a glass of wine. He smiled at me.

'Thanks for the invitation, Sarah. I haven't been to a dinner party in years.'

I took the bottle and moved on to fill the other guests' glasses. Amy wrapped both hands around hers, nursing it like a cup of coffee. I felt hungry, even though I'd eaten two packets of crisps and a Mars bar before coming to ensure the meal didn't distract me from Neil. I excused myself and walked to Mary's bathroom.

Unsurprisingly, the room was spotless. Mary was a nice middle-class girl at heart, and no matter how dishevelled her dress, I knew she wouldn't be able to cope with an untidy toilet. The only evidence of recent use was a ring of soapy water around the sink's plug-hole. I stared at my feet as I urinated, wondering whether Neil would like my new black mules.

Mary had left a small basket of pot-pourri on top of the toilet. Pushed into the pink and brown flakes were the Minnie Mouse sunglasses Mary'd won on the pier. I ran my hands down my outfit, checking for pockets I knew weren't there. Then I stretched forward the waistband of my skirt and tucked the glasses into the front of my knickers, hiding the bulge with my belt.

As the flush died down, I could hear Neil talking to Mary. Until now, I'd felt little towards Neil, seeing him only as an opportunity for a few enjoyable evenings. Now, ridiculously, I felt terrified. I adjusted my skirt and walked downstairs.

Neil was wearing the suit Paul had bought for him when he first came to Weston, only with a black polo neck instead of a shirt. The combination was better suited to a man of Henry's age, but Neil's long neck and serious face helped him get away with it.

The first course was a cold soup Mary had wanted to cook because she'd never done it before. I couldn't identify the taste, but the spearmint colour suggested peas or leeks.

'What's this called?' Ben asked.

'Soup,' Vanessa told him.

'No, it's got a special name.'

'Vicky something?' Amy suggested.

'That's right. It's French,' said Ben.

Neil seemed distracted, not saying anything to me and offering only brief comments to the general conversation. Although Mary had told me how much Neil liked me, I couldn't help thinking he was becoming reluctant now I was going after him. Maybe he'd been charmed by my aloofness, and felt intimidated by this direct approach.

'How are you supposed to eat soup?' Ben asked, looking across the table to Neil. 'I know you're only supposed to go in one direction, but is it towards or away from your body?'

'Who cares, Mr Etiquette,' Mary told him. 'Eat it any way you like.'

Lee appeared after the soup. Amy sat up and smiled at him. He didn't respond. He was wearing a green and white bike jacket and his hair was oilier than usual. He'd brought two bottles of Kiwi-Lemon 20/20.

'Were they out of Thunderbirds?' Mary asked. 'Or did you pinch those off a tramp on your way here?'

Lee ignored her, taking the empty seat between Mary and Amy. He looked at Vanessa, then at Neil. Vanessa stared back.

'I'm afraid you've missed the soup,' Mary told him, 'but that's what happens when you're late. I'll make it up by serving the next course to you first. Come on, Sarah, I need your help to carry it in.'

In the kitchen, Mary asked me how I was doing.

'You can see how I'm doing,' I told her. 'He refuses to speak.'

She laughed and handed me two plates of chicken. I carried them into the lounge. I served Lee first and then Vanessa. Mary brought in the bowl of salad and filled up a few glasses of wine.

'Mary,' said Ben, 'would you mind if I changed the music?'

'No, that's fine, the CDs are in the cupboard beneath the stereo.'

I leaned across to Neil.

'You're very quiet.'

'I'm just a bit tired, that's all. I didn't get much sleep last night.'

'How come?'

'It's hard to relax in my flat.'

'Is that because of the couple?'

'What couple?'

'The couple you live with.'

'Who told you about that?'

'Mary.'

Ben selected his CD. Jimi Hendrix. It seemed obvious that this was the sort of music he would like. I tried to remember what the music had been like in the club when we met him. I wish I had more knowledge of music. When I was younger, my female friends used to double their record collection with every new boyfriend. I'd always wanted a man who'd teach me about music, but all of my lovers either didn't care what they listened to, or had narrow, boring tastes. Even Charlie, for all his alternative ways, had little grasp on popular music, preferring to listen to Brahms.

I went back out into the kitchen and Mary and I brought in the remaining plates. The break between courses had served its purpose, with the guests falling into separate conversations. I was worried about the attention Vanessa was giving Ben, and I could sense that this was irritating both Lee and Mary. Amy responded by trying to draw Lee into conversation, but he kept staring at Vanessa, poking at his food a few times before giving up and lighting a cigarette.

The wine was beginning to influence my behaviour, and I felt an urgent need to put my hand on Neil's leg. I fiddled with my glass instead. I wondered how sober he was, but knew better than to ask. I smiled at him and tried to pick up our previous conversation: 'So why don't you move out?'

'It's still a nice flat,' he told me, 'even with the couple. They've got everything. And it's not as if they treat me badly. Besides, I'd never find anywhere else that was as cheap.'

The wine sauce was too thick and had set round the meat like cheese. I scraped it off with my knife, tugging up small coils of chicken between the serrations. Even without the waxy sauce, I couldn't stomach the meat. I asked Lee for a cigarette. He didn't hear me. Neil produced a box of Embassy's. I tried to remember if this was his usual brand. I find it hard to concentrate on Neil. Usually I can judge exactly what effect sleeping with someone will have. A quick spot of mental arithmetic, and the decision whether it's worth it. And after the deliberation, the most delicious period is often the masturbatory anticipation before the event itself. But every time I'd gone to bed to think about Neil, none of my fantasy tricks had worked. I began with Neil's head, then, as always, connected it to Paul's body, but as soon as I tried to go further, to scroll through my memorybank of young men's members, I couldn't find anything that would fit. And whereas in the past, the fun of selecting a cock usually led me into a non-specific finger frenzy, this time I turned back to the remembered sensation of Charlie's come on my breasts.

Ben smiled at Mary. 'This is a lovely dinner. Thanks.'

'Makes a change from microwave meals,' Neil added. 'Are we going anywhere afterwards?'

'That'd be nice,' said Vanessa. 'The Imperial or something.'

Amy was watching Lee. I wondered if Ben knew how much trouble he was causing. I tried to catch Vanessa's eye, but she was giving Ben her full attention. I'd changed my mind about her being an equal. I've never been impressed by that kind of attention seeking, and would have felt Lee was completely within in his rights if he'd stood up and punched her in the face.

Amy asked Lee if he wanted some more wine. He shrugged. She filled his glass. The bottle passed round the table. Vanessa leaned in closer to Ben.

'Are you drunk?' she asked.

He looked embarrassed. I could tell Lee had had enough. He finished his cigarette and deliberately squashed it against his plate.

'Vanessa,' he said, 'would you come outside with me?'

She stared at him. 'Why?'

'I've got something I need to tell you.'

'Tell me then. I don't want to go outside.'

'Just for a minute, Vanessa, that's all. Don't embarrass me.'

Vanessa stood up, pulled her serviette from her top and dropped it onto her plate. She carried her drink with her and the two of them walked back out to the staircase. Mary looked at me and I shrugged, wanting to tell her not to worry but feeling scared myself.

'Fucking hell,' said Amy.

I looked at her. 'Is it serious?'

'I don't know,' she sighed. 'Probably.'

'What's the problem?' Ben asked, his voice hesitant. 'Did I do something?'

'Don't worry,' Amy told him, 'it's not your fault.'

'They're a very tempestuous couple,' I explained.

No one seemed interested in finishing their food. I gestured to Mary and we cleared the plates. I'd told her not to bother with dessert so we just brought some cheese in and two fresh bottles of wine. Lee's 20/20 still stood on the table.

'Does anyone want this?' Mary asked. 'Or shall I pour it down the sink?'

'Save it for Lee,' Amy suggested. 'I expect he'll be glad of a drink.'

I sat down. Minnie Mouse's ears dug into my flesh. Ben was the only one who made any attempt to eat, stretching his arm out for a plate of crackers. I felt a silent energy coming from Neil and knew he had something to say about this. We waited in silence until the door opened. Lee's hand was wrapped around his neck. His pale face floated back to the table. He reached for a serviette. As he pressed the tissue to his neck, I noticed spots of red.

'What happened?' Amy asked.

'She freaked out and cut me with her wine glass.'

'Are you okay?' said Mary. 'Should I call someone?'

'No, don't worry. It isn't deep.'

'Where's Vanessa?'

'I don't know. She ran down the street crying and screaming rubbish. She'll come back.'

'I'll go look for her,' I told them.

'She'll come back,' he repeated.

I ignored him and stood up. Ben and Amy looked at each other. I walked across the room, fingers crossed. It took five steps before Neil said: 'I'll come with you.'

Success.

5

Saturday

My mum told me about dark chocolate. Every month I'd find a Fry's bar on my pillow a few nights before it started. As a child I thought it would ease the hurt, like sucking barley sugars when you go through tunnels in a train. Now it's a craving which precedes the pain inside, and I'm sure the only way I'll know I'm pregnant will be if I stop wanting my chocolate rations.

I still hadn't had my first night with Neil, and worried at his age he might still be squeamish. We'd found Vanessa in a pub three streets from Mary's flat, scaring the regulars with her sobs. It'd taken the rest of the evening to get anything coherent out of her, and after all that effort neither Neil nor I felt in the mood for progressing further. Our parting had been old fashioned and romantic, his gallantry surprising me. I'd planned to remain pragmatic about our coupling, not wanting Neil to construct anything epic around a few summer fucks, but now I found myself relishing the slow pace. And when Neil asked when he'd see me next, a Saturday-night date seemed the most appropriate choice. Besides, there should have been four clear days before I came on.

For once Neil wasn't wearing a suit, and his springy ginger hair was freshly washed. I breathed in as he kissed me, pleased by the scent of his medicated shampoo. It was a clean smell, so much nicer than Henry's hair oil or Paul's wet-look gel. Beneath the freshness, I noticed the perennial adolescent fragrance of amber Lynx, the same deodorant that I had once sprayed beneath my sheets. The harsh odour reminded me of evenings passed in bus shelters and a familiar trickle down the first joint of my right hand. I smiled at him. He offered me a stick of gum. I shook my head. He slipped one into his mouth and started chewing.

'Did you see *Blind Date*?' he asked.

'I don't have a television.'

'Couldn't you go down to the TV room?'

'It's horrible on a Saturday. There's families who get there at five and stay until midnight.'

'I love Saturday television, especially *Blind Date*. It wasn't that good tonight, but it's fun to watch it before you go out. Where do you want to go?'

'I don't mind.'

'The Star?' he suggested.

'Are you serious?'

He smiled. 'Why not?'

Paul once told me that he would go to any pub in Weston except The Star. It was the only time he'd admitted any weakness, and I'd found it hard to picture somewhere Paul felt scared of. I'd even considered going there alone, just to get a glimpse inside, thinking it was probably safer for women than men. I looked at Neil and wondered if it was naïveté or courage that kept him out of harm.

'Have you been there before?'

'Of course.'

'I thought it was rough.'

'The Star? Maybe on a Friday, but I've never had any trouble. Do you want to go somewhere else?'

'No,' I told him, 'that's fine.'

Vanessa's condition had been easy to diagnose. Her brain wanted rid of Lee but her body refused to let him go. This was the fourth time she'd flirted with someone else in front of him, and as usual Lee had smugly watched, waiting for her to give in and return to him. She couldn't understand why it was so difficult. She'd slept with plenty of men before Lee and had no fear of one-night stands. But knowing that as soon as she took someone else Lee would be gone for good made it impossible for her to make this leap. Wednesday night's lunge with the wine glass had been as much as she could muster, and she knew it wasn't convincing.

Two summers ago, Paul decided to extend his market by trying to sell his neon signs to pubs. He sent me out to pitch the displays, but in two weeks I didn't make a single sale. I just didn't understand publicans like I did restaurateurs. They held back too many secrets, and were impossible to intimidate. When Neil introduced me to the owner of The Star, I could tell he was like his brothers from his stern, shiny face and the way he avoided my eye as he poured me a Tia Maria.

We found a table by the quiz machine. I was still nervous, worried the locals had only pretended to accept Neil while they saved his kicking to liven up a dull night. Neil called over a pale-faced man with shoulder-length blond hair and a ratty moustache.

'Jim, this is Sarah. How's your mouth, Jim?'

'Not so bad.'

'Jim was really drunk the other night and he ate some glass for a bet,' Neil explained. 'How many stitches did you need?'

'Eight.'

'But it's okay now?'

'Yeah, it's okay. The only problem is that if I suck down on the wound I get this taste in my mouth like I've been eating shit.'

'When are you going on holiday?' Neil asked.

'Tuesday.'

'Okay, you listen to me, on Monday morning you go down to the chemist and you ask them to give you some anti-inflammatory pills. If you've got the taste of shit in your mouth that means you've got an abscess coming. If you get an abscess while you're in Spain you won't be able to do anything and you'll have this pain in your mouth that'll feel like someone's punching you in the jaw over and over again.'

'Have you had one then?' I asked, impressed by his knowledge.

'I had one that ran along beneath my teeth. They had to pull out a tooth and stick a tube into my gum to drain off the fluid. That's what started me off spitting. I used to hate spitting, but I had this brown poison inside me and I had to get rid of it.'

'My spit's green,' said Jim, laughing.

'Well then, what other signs do you need. You're not supposed to have anything green inside your body.'

'Ah fuck it,' said Jim, 'I can't be bothered. I'll just have another glass of sangria.'

My fingers went to my lips. I'd never thought of my body like that, never contemplated that the blood I carry around inside me could turn into poison. Jim patted Neil on the shoulder and stood up, staggering back to his friends. The other people in the pub didn't look that intimidating, and there were several couples enjoying intimate drinks. I knew much worse places than this in Weston, and I couldn't understand why Paul had singled it out.

'Do you remember that first night when you stayed with me?'

'Of course.'

'I really wanted you to stay in my room. I was so pleased when Paul suggested it.'

'Don't lie,' he told me, 'I saw the look you gave him.'

His directness embarrassed me. 'Okay, I wasn't happy about you seeing my room, but I liked listening to your breathing.'

'My breathing?'

I nodded. 'It's nice to hear someone else breathing in the dark, don't you think?'

He laughed. 'I hadn't really thought about it.'

Neil drank from his glass. I couldn't believe how much power I'd granted him. He was controlling everything, right down to the pace of our conversation. I felt a kamikaze urge to break through his reserve, and tried once more to spark his interest: 'When I was a child, I was obsessed with the idea of having someone else in my bed. I made up imaginary friends who lived under my sheets.'

Neil smiled. 'I used to have an imaginary audience.'

'Watching when you're having sex?'

'No, when I was a kid. I used to think everything I did was a TV show. I planned every day like a television schedule. Nine o'clock, Neil wakes up. Nine thirty, Neil has breakfast. I still feel it sometimes.' He drew breath. 'How old were you when you first slept with someone?'

'Slept as in sex?'

'No. Slept as in slept.'

'Ten or eleven. I used to go to sleepovers with the girls in my class. I really liked it until one of them tried to touch me up. Since then I've hated sharing beds with girls. But I've never lost my original dream and I still wish I could go to bed with lots of people at the same time. Nothing sexual, just lots of friends dreaming with their heads next to each other.'

'Is this your way of telling me you don't want to have sex with me?'

'No, not at all,' I told him, feeling nervous. 'I love sex.'

I didn't realise how high my voice had risen until I noticed a man at the next table staring at me. I blushed. Neil laughed. He seemed to have doubled in size. I felt like a child. He offered me a cigarette. I shook my head, a petty stab at independence.

He smiled. 'I think the couple I live with would like me to watch them in bed together. Maybe even join them, I don't know. When they're having sex, they're really noisy, and I think they probably have a fantasy where I go in to complain and I can't believe how beautiful they look so I take off my clothes and join them in bed.'

'Perhaps we can do that tonight.'

'Perhaps.'

I'd planned to stay sober tonight. I can't stand sex when I'm dehydrated, I lose all enthusiasm. But Neil seemed excited every time I accepted another glass, and I got caught up in the evening. Outside in the still humid atmosphere, I could feel the beginnings of a headache beating in tandem with the pain in my back. Maybe some food would sort me out.

'Fish and chips?'

Neil stared at me, as if judging whether to grant my request. 'Yeah, you're right,' he said. 'We need something to soak it up if we're going to last the distance.'

We started walking towards The Cod Plaice. There are other chip shops in Weston, but anyone who stays here more than a few weeks soon realises it's the only place for an afterdark snack. The night was hot in a sneaky way, the warmth seeming to come from inside instead of the sun. My legs glowed as if I'd just shaved with a blunt razor. Neil deliberately slowed his pace.

'Would you ever get like Vanessa?'

'Depends what you mean. I've felt desperate before.'

'But could you cut someone like that?'

'Maybe. If I was scared enough.'

'Lee didn't seem that scary.'

'Vanessa's not afraid of Lee. She's afraid of herself.'

'Still. That's no reason to mutilate someone.'

I laughed. 'It wasn't serious.'

'She stabbed him in the neck.'

'She didn't mean to. It was a gesture of frustration.'

He stared at me, open mouthed. Neil's most youthful feature was his large front teeth, their precarious prominence seeming to invite someone to smash them out. I was surprised at the emotion this argument seemed to be provoking. I sensed he had something to tell me, but I didn't like to pressure him. Then he said: 'I'm sorry. I can't understand that.'

'How can you say that?' I asked. 'For Christ's sake, your friend Jim did himself worse damage for a bet.'

'That's completely different.'

I took his hand. 'Let's not argue.'

'What?' he asked. 'Why not?'

I could tell Neil was excited and wanted to carry on, but I knew I was only fighting because I'd drunk too much, and I could hear a strident tone entering my voice. I hate the way men can switch like that. One minute they're shouting at you and the next they expect a kiss. Charlie used to get an erection every time we had an argument.

We continued to the chip shop in silence. Neil waited in the queue while I sat on the wall outside. I tried to breathe deeply, but that only made me feel sicker. The smell of the freshly fried food made me wonder if I really did want to eat. I straightened my hair and rubbed my face, pressing my thumbs against my eyelids. I stayed like that until Neil returned with the food.

'So,' he said, 'where next?'

I opened my packet of fish and chips and looked down at the curling yellow tail. 'That's up to you. Is it okay to go back to your flat?'

'Yeah, probably, but I thought we might go somewhere different.'

'Like where?'

'What I thought was,' he began, checking my face after every word, 'this is embarrassing, but I'm drunk so what the fuck. It's always been a fantasy of mine to have sex on the beach.'

'Oh.'

'What? Don't you want to?'

'No, no,' I said, thinking quickly, 'it's not that. I think it would be lovely, but I don't think tonight would be a good night for it. I'd be a bit scared, what with people walking along the beach after they've been to the pub. Let's save it for another night. We could take a blanket down and find a nice spot, do it properly.'

He smiled. 'Okay, then. So, for tonight, do you want to come home with me?'

I nodded, and stood up. Neil was even more fastidious with his food than me, and I wondered if there might be a male equivalent to Paul's theory about how women eat chips. He had long thin fingers, and I felt nervous about the length of his nails. I would be very selective about what I'd let him do to me tonight.

'Oh,' he said, 'there might be a problem. I know it's stupid but I honestly didn't think about it until I was in the pub, and I'm afraid this was all they had.'

He reached into his jeans and pulled out a small black cardboard box. I took it from him. Three flavours. Lager and Lime. Chocolate. And Curry. For entertainment only. Not to be used as a barrier. I've never understood who these things are aimed at. Surely if you're buying contraceptives from a pub, you're more likely to need protection than a sordid giggle. I tried to imagine the ideal novelty condom customer. Some fat man with a flat cap taking them home to shock the wife.

'It's okay,' I said. 'I've got something.'

I'd brought three condoms and a femidom. I'd never used the latter before, but I thought it might be useful to hide the blood. I'd practised putting it in the day before and it seemed okay, but I worried it might prove too fiddly in my current state.

Before Neil put his key in the slot, his housemate opened the door. She was wrapped in a stiff purple blanket that seemed better suited to hanging on a wall or covering a chair. Her legs and shoulders revealed a tan that suggested membership at the solarium beneath March Entertainments. She had shoulder-length brown hair and sunken eyes.

'I told you,' she shouted to her husband, 'Neil's brought a woman home.'

'Sarah, this is Colette,' said Neil. 'Colette, Sarah.'

'Come in, both of you. We've got a great video.'

Neil walked past Colette into the living area. A man with the same long curly hair as Colette was sitting on the sofa. He was wearing a pair of black satin shorts and was equally tanned.

'This is Jase,' she said. 'You won't get much out of him while the video's on. He's a real movie buff. Would you like something to eat?'

'No, I'm fine,' Neil told her.

'Sarah?'

'No thanks.'

'Coffee then? Come on, you ought to have something.'

We accepted two coffees and Colette left us with Jase. He pointed at the screen with the remote. 'Jeff Fahey,' he told us, 'he's really underrated.'

I couldn't tell if the musky odour was coming from the room or Jason. He had the same shiny, puckered nipples as Charlie, although his body was too scrawny for me. He stared at the television with a disturbingly intense concentration, given that the film seemed to be nothing more than a series of explosions. I had no idea if Jeff Fahey was an actor or a stuntman, and could see no reason why anyone would go to the trouble of even underrating him.

Neil seemed nervous in Jason's presence, and kept looking suspiciously at me, as if trying to gauge whether I found him attractive. I could tell he regretted telling me about his belief the couple wanted to sleep with him, and saw how this hippyish atmosphere might intimidate him.

Colette returned with the coffees. I could sense she wanted to talk but was worried about disturbing her boyfriend. As the video progressed I could see why Jason watched it so intensely. The images were so fast moving that a second's lapse in attention rendered the whole sequence incomprehensible. Colette sat at the table and rolled a joint. Watching her do this made me think of Lee and Vanessa and I wondered why I didn't spend my time like they did, getting stoned and hiding in front of the television.

Halfway through my coffee, Neil tapped me on the shoulder. I nodded and followed him to his bedroom. I could see why he felt he had no privacy from the couple. In the wall of his room there was a large rectangular hole like a serving hatch with no doors. 'I'm sure the minute we start doing anything they'll pop their heads through,' he told me, and I laughed, wanting him to relax.

'I just need to go to the bathroom,' I told him.

'Okay,' he said, 'it's next to the kitchen.'

Colette looked up from the television as I passed them.

She smiled at me. I wasn't sure about Jason, but Colette seemed nicer than Neil had suggested. She seemed like a sister, or a liberated mother, and I expected her to offer to lend me some KY jelly.

Neil sat on the edge of his bed, naked except for a pair of cherry-red boxer shorts. He was more muscular than I imagined, and I felt pleased his chest and shoulders were free of spots. For a ginger-haired man, his skin looked surprisingly healthy. His body seemed closer to Henry's than Paul's, with the same scrappy wisps of hair around his ankles and along his inner thighs. His big toes were the nicest surprise, round and chunky like the teat of a dummy.

He placed a piece of red material over the bedside lamp. I sat on the edge of the bed and unlaced my caramel-coloured shoes. Neil put his hand on my shoulder, preventing me from undressing further.

'I've waited so long to see you naked,' he told me. 'Let me tremble a little longer.'

His hand reached up under my skirt. Inexperienced fingers felt exquisite after so many confident gropes, and for once my skin felt like tissue paper instead of bacon rind. He pulled down my knickers and stroked my cunt through the material of my skirt. Anxious about him dislodging the femidom, I moved his fingers away from my labia and up against my clit.

We fell back onto the bed and I stroked his thighs, reaching up to feel his weight before peeling off his boxer shorts. As much as I wanted to touch him there, I felt silly when I did, like an old lady testing fruit.

His cotton-blend boxers sprang back over his shape, and I felt my usual urge to stake out the space between my lover's legs. I let my hair droop down over his testicles and started nuzzling him. I felt like a vampire as I licked his perineum, knowing Neil would be disturbed if he knew the extent of my deviant tastes. How could I explain that if I had my way I'd cut a square of skin from the back of his balls to the opening of his arse and take it to bed with me every night.

I could feel him rearing and tried to placate his desire by sucking his average-sized cock. He smelt so soaped, and my tastebuds were grateful for the introductory droplets of sperm emerging beneath the pressure of my tongue. He pulled at my shoulders and I followed his demands, moving up on top of him and guiding his cock towards the polyurethane target. I used two fingers to open myself for him, surprised at how easily he slipped inside. Most of my first times have started with an unsatisfactory shuffling, forcing me to resist until my partner gets into my rhythm. Neil's first few motions were slyly coaxing, and I hardly noticed him straightening the path towards my cervix.

I hadn't expected Neil to set the pace. I was older, I was on top. But he retained an intent control, moving quickly but managing not to hurt me. My cunt was unaccustomed to such gentle, generous energy, and his rounded cock felt more like a vibrator than a human organ. I checked his eyes and moved my fingers down to touch myself, hoping this wouldn't shock him. He moaned and arched his stomach, granting me more room to masturbate. It was so good that for once I closed my eyes out of pleasure instead of to avoid looking at the body beneath me. Just as I was beginning to feel the first flutters of an approaching orgasm, he slowed down, prolonging the build-up and giving him the breath to talk to me: 'Do you know when I first started wanting you?'

'Tell me.'

'That day we went to Clevedon together. You looked so beautiful that day. You always look beautiful, but usually in a stand-offish way. That day was the first time I thought I had a chance with you. Every item you were wearing seemed designed to turn me on. I could see the shape of your breasts so clearly beneath the material of your top. Your pale skirt seemed so simple yet so sexy too, and it really showed off the beauty of your legs. And even though it was so hot you were wearing tights, which seemed weird until we were sitting in that woman's office and I looked down and I realised they were stockings. I've always thought of you like that when I've masturbated about you, always imagined my hands slipping up under that dress to touch your cunt.'

Young men are so verbose. I don't usually like being talked at during sex, but Neil's adeptness at matching the rhythm of his hips to his words made me even more desperate. Every breath plundered from the bottom of my lungs. He gripped my hips and I knew his sperm was squirting into the femidom. Scared of losing my own orgasm, my walls squeezed tighter and shook the last required thrusts out of him, triggering a full minute of melting contractions.

He fell asleep before me, and I tried to arrange myself into a loving position so he'd have good dreams. I managed to join him before long, but by 4 a.m. backache and stomach pains had disrupted my rest. I needed some food and my pills. The latter were in my jacket pocket, but food was more difficult. I found my top on the floor and walked out to the kitchen. I was praying Colette had a secret chocolate store, but all I found were hazelnut bars and nutrition supplements. I settled on an apple and bit into it, trying to suck the juice into the holes created by the pain.

I sensed a presence behind me. Colette stood in the doorway, pressing her head against the wooden frame.

'I'm sorry,' I told her, 'period pains.'

'I'll make you a hot drink,' she said. 'What would you like?'

'I don't suppose you have any hot chocolate?'

'Of course we do,' she said, 'it's my favourite. Anything else?'

'Just some water for my pills.'

I sat at the table while she prepared the drink. Colette was wearing a black silk dressing gown and I wanted to feel the smooth material against my hot skin. There seemed something heartbreaking about her movements around the kitchen and I wanted to tell her about my life because I thought she would understand. But instead she brought the drinks across and we sat in silence until they were finished and then went to bed.

ʃ

Sunday

I awoke early. My pills wore off around six, and it took more effort to keep my eyes closed than wake up. For once I hadn't been pushed to the side of the bed and I felt touched Neil had held me all night. His skin looked healthier close up, and I liked stroking his aristocratic eyebrows.

Obscure economics textbooks lay scattered across the floor, alongside sheets of file paper covered in blue biro scribblings. It seemed Neil was eager to return to his degree. I've never regretted leaving university, but I do sometimes wonder what might have happened to me if I'd studied properly. I just like the idea of filling exercise books with secret writings, being able to communicate in academic code.

I'd expected Neil's suits to be hanging under plastic dust covers, but he'd left his jackets over the back of an armchair. I wondered if this was Colette's and Jason's influence.

I always feel uneasy when I see someone else's room. Too much life too close up. Just knowing that the hollow in Neil's pillow came from the weight of his head gave me the creeps, and made me think how amazing it is that any of us survive any longer than a day.

Neil wriggled and let me free. I moved across the mattress and wondered what I should do. My back was too painful to lie there much longer, but I didn't want to disturb Neil, and although I doubted Colette or Jason arose before midday, I still felt uneasy about walking around their home.

I decided to take some more pills. I tiptoed to the kitchen and eased the tap on, cringing as the flow of the water came accompanied with the clanks of the plumbing. Hoping that everyone was still asleep, I sat at the kitchen table and placed two pills on my morning-furred tongue.

Neil awoke around nine. He smiled at me and I wondered if we'd make love again. My period pain had obliterated my hangover, and my tablets had reduced that throbbing to a manageable knot in the middle of my forehead. He smelt so much nicer now he'd allowed his body to sweat a little, and as I kissed him my tongue lingered around his lips.

He pushed me back and stared at me. 'You seem different now I've slept with you.'

'So do you,' I said, rubbing my legs against his.

'Do you think people will be able to tell?'

'What people?'

'People in work.'

'I don't understand,' I said, staring at him. 'Mary knows about it, and I don't want Paul to find out.'

'I thought you had an open relationship.'

'We have, up to a point.' I stared at him. 'You haven't said anything, have you?'

He smiled. I couldn't tell if he was being naïve or just teasing me. Either way I didn't like it.

'No, don't worry,' he said. 'I'll keep your secret.'

'It's not just my secret,' I told him, my voice rising, 'Paul won't be happy to find out you've been fucking me.'

'So I should start looking for another job?'

'It's not the job you should worry about. Paul's got contacts, you know.'

'Come on,' he protested, 'surely he wouldn't risk that.'

'Maybe not, but I can't see you getting away without a fight.'

He looked away. I felt stupidly upset, and embarrassed by my boasting about Paul. I had no idea what he'd do if he found out about me and Neil, but I didn't like losing the drama of my betrayal. I stroked his armpit.

'Do you wish we hadn't done it?' I asked.

'No, of course not,' he said, speaking quickly, 'I just didn't realise it was such a big deal.'

I drew breath. Neil noticed, but I didn't want him to realise how easily he'd hurt me, so I smiled and ran my fingers through his hair. I didn't feel like making love any more and I could see Neil wanted me to leave. I tried not to read too much into his behaviour, thinking it was the usual self-disgust men seemed to get whenever they sleep with someone new. In my experience, these emotions had less to do with their feelings about their conquest than the size of their ego. Small wonder Neil was so testy.

I don't blame Charlie. The Pygmalion instinct must be hard to resist. I'd known from the outset that Charlie would be attracted to Lesley, and after the virtuous way he'd handled Melissa, it was obvious the urge to misbehave would soon return. I even told him I didn't mind if he slept with her, as long as he promised me it wasn't serious. But somehow he'd convinced himself that our relationship was a compromise, and my offer only increased his need to escape. It's true that I wouldn't tell Charlie I loved him, but only because back then those words really meant something to me. I don't regret my reticence, even though I've said those words to everyone I've slept with since. I'm sure Lesley told Charlie she loved him every single day.

When I got back to the guest house, Sylvia was sitting in reception.

'Isn't this your day for seeing Henry?' she asked.

'It used to be.'

'Oh, I didn't realise you'd fallen out. Have you had lunch?'

'Not yet.'

'Could I treat you? Say no if you've got other plans. Only at the end of a week spent cooking for other people, it makes a change to have someone else do it for you. And I don't like eating alone.'

'That would be lovely,' I told her. 'Just give me a moment to freshen up.'

'Of course,' she said, and went back to her magazine.

Sylvia has the same car as my mother. I hadn't noticed this when I'd ridden with her before, and now I'd made the connection I wasn't going to dwell on it. My mother and landlady had nothing else in common, and I think my mother Sandra would be repelled by the odd creature who offers me bed and board. Her hennaed hair suggests respectability, but there is something accepting and secretive about her, a strange seaside creepiness which makes me wonder if she has another life running a bordello or dressing up in latex to pose as a mascot for gay men.

'Thank you for agreeing to eat with me, Sarah. It seems a shame that we don't get to spend much time together.'

'Thank you for inviting me. All I had was a Pot Noodle.'

'Is that what you were going to eat?' she asked, her thin lips crinkling into an odd smile. 'I don't suppose you have much time for shopping, what with two jobs and everything.'

She spotted a space up ahead and parked the car. 'Can you get us a cheap meal in any of these restaurants, dear? Any loyal customers?'

'Paul would kill me if I used my connections,' I told her. 'He's the only one who's allowed to ask for discounts.'

'Never mind. We'll have to rely on our feminine charms. Loosen your top button, dear.'

Sylvia asked for a table in the smoking section and placed a packet of red Dunhills between us on the table.

'Feel free to help yourself.'

'Thanks, but I've quit.'

'Have you quit? That's brave. Don't let me tempt you.'

'Actually, would you mind if I had one? There's no harm in the odd one now and again, is there?'

'No harm at all. Help yourself.'

Behind Sylvia's head were two paintings of women lost in woods. The first woman was surrounded by blue darkness, her eyes defiantly avoiding whatever lurked beyond the restrictions of the frame. At first it seemed as if the woman wanted to escape the painting, but as I focused in on her forced smile, I realised we were supposed to follow her and recognised the picture for what it was: a rescue fantasy in garish oils.

The second painting lacked the tension of the first, presenting a Bardot lookalike happy in the middle of an orange copse. Her coy smile had none of the urgency of her endangered sister, and the invitation seemed aimed only at those who wanted to accept it. Anyone who looked at the first painting would be forced to acknowledge it, even if only to wonder why something so tacky should trouble them. The second picture was happy to hang ignored.

'You're in a world of your own, aren't you?' Sylvia said. 'Are you worrying about Henry?'

'No, I'm sorry, I was looking at the paintings behind you.'

Sylvia looked over her shoulder. 'Revolting, aren't they? I think they're even more unpleasant than the ones with the crying children. You don't see so many of them around these days, but at one time there were a couple in every guest house in Weston. Except mine, of course. We had reproductions of Van Gogh and Monet. I remember this one landlord who employed an artist to paint a picture of him in the same style so he could put it up between his copies of the two women. He was so proud, but it looked ridiculous. This man with a pipe and a mustard cardigan lost in the woods with two Castilian maidens.'

She laughed at the memory. Her small eyes urged me to open up, and I remembered how scared I felt when she came to my room. I was genuinely glad of her company today, pleased for any excuse not to think about Neil, but I couldn't help feeling like I was at dinner with my headmistress. No topic of conversation seemed appropriate. I knew if I relaxed she would too, but I felt an irrational fear that if I didn't exercise the utmost self-control, I would start babbling obscenities.

A waitress came to take our orders. Sylvia smiled conspiratorially at me.

'What shall we have then? Do you feel like pushing the boat out?'

I looked at the menu. 'I always have the same thing when I come here. I feel like having something really different.'

'I don't know if you'll find anything that exotic. Would you like to go somewhere else?'

'No, it's okay, I know what I want. Sausage, beans and chips. And a large Coke.'

'Bread and butter?' the waitress inquired.

'Yes, thanks, and can I have a straw for the Coke?'

The waitress laughed and turned to Sylvia.

'The lamb,' she said, 'and a tea.'

Sylvia waited until the waitress had returned to the counter and then leaned across.

'I knew Henry,' she said. 'I didn't like to say anything before in case it turned out to be your big romance, but there's no harm in me telling you now.

'I was one of the first women he courted. It was my mother's idea. That was the worst thing about the whole experience. He'd come round ages before the time we'd agreed, just so he could sit in the lounge talking to Mother. She'd make him hold her hand as he spoke, leaning against his shoulder as if she was hard of hearing. Then we'd go out to dances or the pictures and he'd hardly say two words all evening. Do you know how I found out he'd had enough of me? My mother called me into the lounge on a Sunday after church and told me, "Listen, don't get upset, but Henry won't be visiting any more."

'I'm not making a fuss. It was years ago and I'm sure I'm not the only woman to have had her hopes dashed, but Henry was the first man I gave myself to, and Mother knew that. She expected me to hear this news without saying anything. I couldn't even tell my sisters in case word got round that I wasn't intact any more, and she was talking about it as if it was a business transaction.'

Sylvia put such bitter emphasis onto these last two words that I felt scared she was about to burst into sobs. I knew she expected me to follow her story with a description of my relationship with Henry, but our experiences seemed so different that I felt as if I was being forced to empathise with some alien tragedy.

'It sounds so Victorian,' I said, 'I can't believe things were like that.'

'They weren't, in most places,' she said, 'but that's because in most places there are other forces to regulate things.'

'I don't understand.'

'Okay, when you were a little girl, did you feel *stirrings*?'

'Of course.'

'And what did you do about it?'

I blushed, embarrassed to be talking about this with Sylvia. 'The same as everyone else. I fantasised, I had crushes.'

'But you didn't actually *do* anything?'

'Not with someone else.'

'Why not?'

'I was scared.'

'Exactly. But imagine being a teenage girl and having all those desires and knowing that all your friends are going down to the beach and meeting strangers and making love in the sand and it's not horrible and no one knows about it. Wouldn't you want to go? And if you were someone's mother or someone's boyfriend, wouldn't you want to make sure your little girl stayed at home?'

She sounded so impassioned, and her fervour worried me. I remembered her telling me we were so much alike and felt irritated that she saw me as some kind of cause. I wondered what she thought about my lifestyle and if she ever envied me. Her angry face made me want to tell her that going down to the beach at midnight was no more liberating than staying at home. I wanted to shake her and tell her to give up all this stupid emotion and stop feeling so needlessly aggrieved. But I just nodded and took another cigarette.

I didn't manage to get rid of Sylvia until late afternoon, when she had to prepare the light supper she offers her weekend guests. The afternoon had done nothing to calm my nerves, and I felt full of nervous energy. I decided to go for a walk. I walked without a destination in mind, knowing only that I wanted to avoid the Grand Pier and Sand Bay.

I ended up in a newsagents. I hadn't read a paper since I'd left home, but it seemed just the thing to get me through the evening. I bought *The Mail on Sunday* for news and *The News of the World* for fun. Back at the guest house, I found half a bottle of white wine in the downstairs fridge, filled the bath with bubbles, and hoped that the alcohol would eventually slow me down enough to sleep.

5

Monday

I don't know why I didn't think Iona would answer. It was a fifty-fifty chance, after all, probably eighty-twenty given Paul's temperament. But I'd picked up the phone as if making a business call, dialling the number before I'd considered any possible adverse consequences.

Not that there was any reason why talking to her should be a problem. She wasn't the jealous type, Paul'd told me, and unlike television adulterers, he'd never given me dire warnings about what would happen if I called his house. Perhaps he assumed the idea wouldn't occur to me.

'I'm afraid he's asleep,' she told me. 'Can I take a message?'

'Yes, this is Sarah Patton, from work. Could you tell Paul I won't be coming in today.'

'Okay. Goodbye.'

Her quiet, confident voice annoyed me, and I wanted to add *oh, by the way, if your husband feels like fucking me in the lock-up, I'll be free any time after six*. But she'd already hung up.

I was too irritated to go back to bed and I wondered if

taking a day off had been such a good idea. Work had always been my refuge, and I felt angry at myself for compromising that freedom. I wanted to blame it all on Neil, but I knew it was Henry's fault. Before his offer, I'd been every day without fail. Now that I felt I was doing them a favour by turning up, I found it much harder to get out of bed.

I found a pair of blue leggings and a white T-shirt, and walked to the bathroom. I'd forgotten to take my toothbrush last night, and as I picked it up from the sink I noticed the bristles were damp. I'd rather someone fucked my boyfriend than used my toothbrush. Worse still, the bristles had a faint pink tinge that I knew didn't come from toothpaste. I'm worried enough about my gums without a stranger's blood being mixed in there.

I rubbed the bristles under the running water until I felt safe putting the head in my mouth. I cleaned gingerly, then washed my face. After the brush anxiety, I avoided the communal towel and dried the warm drips with the sleeve of my T-shirt.

As long as I was awake, it seemed worth getting breakfast. I padded across the brown-patterned carpet and down to the dining room. My table was the only one without a waiting orange juice. I didn't usually feel up to food before work, and as I saw the morning faces of the hungry families, I wondered if this was such a good idea. I could sense the other guests staring at my bare feet as they passed between their tables. I nervously checked out the shoes of the family next to me, imagining each sole stamping down onto my toes.

Sylvia backed into the dining room, expertly pirouetting a tray onto the nearest table. I moved into her sight line, craving acknowledgement. She winked at me. I waited while she served the couple from Room Nine.

'We don't usually see you for breakfast,' she said, placing an orange juice before me. 'English or Continental?'

'Continental.'
'No work today?'
'No.'
'Nothing's wrong, I hope.'
'Everything's fine. I just felt like having a little break.'
'Very sensible,' said Sylvia, smiling as she moved on to the next table.

Getting a room in a guest house seemed such a clever idea. It removed all the terror of living alone while at the same time allowing me to ignore the people I lived with. The only other arrangement that would suit me so well was living in a hospital, and unfortunately I didn't meet the physical or mental requirements. Being in a guest house also ensured I wouldn't start talking to teapots and wearing my duvet to formal parties. Returning to my room after breakfast, however, I realised that if I was going to accept Henry's offer, I needed a bigger room. Living in a guest house was fine while I led a disciplined existence, but it was impossible to relax in so small a space. Everything about my room seemed designed to get me out and down to the beach for a stroll. Just staying here after nine o'clock seemed an act of defiance.

I sat on my bed and looked at the telephone, wondering who I could call. When Sylvia found out I was staying with her indefinitely, she insisted I got a phone, but I used it so rarely it was hardly worth the line rental. What about your family, Sylvia asked, surely they'll want to call? I nodded and didn't make a fuss. When I sent my mother my address I'd made it explicit that if she tried to call the guest house, I'd move and never tell her where I'd gone. I told Sylvia she called me every night after work.

Yesterday's newspapers were in a mess by the bed. I'd saved the colour supplements for an idle moment, but hadn't expected to need them so soon. I picked them up and carried them down to the lounge. Two children lay on the floor, fighting over a game of Battleships. A man about Henry's age sat by the bookcase, reading the *Express*. The television was tuned to HTV, a quiz show. Every now and again the old man answered one of the questions from behind his newspaper.

I sat by the window, pulling back the net curtain to check on the weather. The clouds were low today, almost hidden behind the roofs of the other guest houses. It was still hot, and the sunlight made the photographs in my magazine seem glossy and inviting. I watched a young couple whispering to each other in the hallway. The husband's face looked strained as he came into the lounge and rescued the two kids from their game.

The old man folded his newspaper and looked at me.

'You look like Sandy Shaw.'

'Thank you,' I said, ignoring him.

He stood up, and walked to the window. I worried he was about to start a conversation, but he was only looking at the sky. He made an odd low murmur, somewhere between a sigh and a chuckle, and left me to my paper.

It seemed perverse to be sitting indoors, but I knew that once I went outside I'd wander round aimlessly till tea time. I had to catch this restlessness early on. It was time to acknowledge that my newfound anxiety was not due to a period of upheaval, had nothing to do with the largesse of an arrogant old man, and was inspired entirely by the knowledge that for the first time since Charlie, I'd allowed myself to fall in love. That matter settled, I turned to the back of the magazine and read my stars.

Sylvia didn't prepare lunches on weekdays, so after doggedly remaining in my chair all afternoon, I walked into town for some fish and chips. I ate the food on the pier, throwing what I didn't want to the seagulls. The beach doesn't seem so grim when it's hot, and I thought that as long as I walked far enough past the tourist spots, there were worse ways to spend an afternoon than lying in the sun. I began by the donkey rides and walked until I could no longer smell them. I found a small ridge of almost dry sand before the sludge and sandworms started and sat down. I let my hair fall over my face and rolled up the bottom of my leggings. I felt stupid tanning my ankles, but they're the only part of my body that's free from moles, and I don't want to have to worry about skin cancer.

I wondered how many days I could spend like this without getting bored. One of the few teachers I had liked at university had told me that she'd spent the previous four years trying to work out the secret of pleasure. During the first year, she had travelled extensively, rarely spending more than a day in the same place. In the second she had holed up in an American university, devoting every waking moment to the study of great literature. For the third year she'd turned to pleasures of the flesh, seducing every man and woman she came across. Then, in the fourth, she'd become a recluse, reading only glossy magazines and pornography, denying herself any comfort that could not be granted by her own hand. For the fifth, sixth and seventh years of her experiment, she was undertaking a PhD, hoping that everything she'd enjoyed in the last four years could somehow be combined in academia. It wasn't until she stroked my leg that I realised she'd told me this to seduce me, and then I had to inform her that my desires were strictly heterosexual.

I walked back from the beach at five o'clock, thinking that if all else failed I could have a nap before dinner. When I'd been on the dole back at home, it'd been so much easier to fill dead days. I wondered if I'd ever be able to get as nonchalant about time as I'd once been. I guess I'm just not cut out to have my own private fortune.

Paul was sitting in the lounge with Sylvia, waiting for me. My landlady looked nervous, and I could tell she was worrying whether inviting him in had been a good idea. I tried to smile reassuringly.

'Here she is,' Sylvia said, standing up. 'I'll leave you two to it.'

'Where have you been?' he asked.

'The doctor's.'

'Left it a bit late, didn't you?'

'I didn't feel up to it this morning. Besides, unless you're in there at the crack of dawn you don't stand a chance of being seen.'

'Right,' he said, his voice rising, 'anyway, I'm sorry to intrude on your sickness, but I need to talk to you about the pier.'

'Okay.'

'The local news saw the reports in the paper and they want to do a feature on me. I wondered if you'd be prepared to be interviewed.'

'What d'you want me to say?'

'Nothing sycophantic. Just a little background on the business and what you think of the operation.'

'But not the truth, right?' I said, feeling mutinous.

'What?'

'You don't want me to tell them about the unofficial stuff.'

He looked shocked. 'Of course not. What are you talking about?'

'Just making a joke. Sorry.'

'Okay,' he said, not laughing. 'So you think you can handle it?'

'Of course.'

'Great. Will we see you in work tomorrow?'

'I hope so.'

'Good. Anyway, get well soon.'

'Thanks.'

He nodded and left the lounge. A few seconds later, Sylvia reappeared, her lips still anxious.

'Was that okay?' she asked. 'I didn't know if you'd want to see him.'

'It was fine. Thanks, Sylvia.'

I sat down in front of the television. Sylvia switched to the soaps. The Australian burble sounded comforting, and I thought to myself if I did stop working, this was one ritual I could cope with.

'You had a visitor last night,' Adrian told me, removing his glasses and cleaning them with the tail of his bowling top.

'Who?'

He lifted the flap so I could join him behind the counter. 'She didn't leave her name.'

'How old was she?' I asked, thinking of Iona.

'Not old. She was pretty sexy. Blonde. If she's single, tell her about your charming boss.'

'What did you tell her?'

'I told her to come back tonight.'

He turned away to serve the next customer. There was a problem with the sixteenth lane and I went across to sort it out. The men playing were embarrassed when I tried to use the computer to restack the pins, presumably because of the names – fuckman, shitface – they'd typed in for each player. The pin stacker wasn't picking up a skittle in the gutter and I had to go down to rescue it. I like running along the lane divider. It makes me feel like a ball, sent speeding into the gutter by a bad bowler.

The men applauded me as I returned, one making a small bow in my direction. I looked down at my feet, knowing I'd exaggerated the simple operation. Hearing about my visitor had reactivated my earlier restlessness, and on my way back to the counter I broke my vow not to look at the clock.

'It's a real drag tonight, isn't it?'

'The heat, you mean?' asked Adrian. 'It's going to get worse.'

'Not just the heat. Don't you ever get fed up with the job?'

Adrian backed the counter, raising his eyebrows as he looked inside a pair of damp shoes. He rubbed his thumb against his small ginger beard. 'Don't you like it here then?'

'It's okay.'

'I like working at night,' he told me, pushing out his lower lip. 'If I wasn't here, I'd be sitting at home getting depressed. As long as I don't have to get up in the morning, I'm happy.'

He took a canister from the counter and sprayed it into the shoes. I looked down at the plastic keychain stretched across the sagging crotch of his brown work trousers. I could tell he wanted to carry on talking to me, but I knew Vanessa would be cross if I broke down the barrier she'd placed between us.

The lanes were full and the new customers were waiting in the café area. I watched a man bowling alone on the eleventh lane. I couldn't understand why anyone would want to bowl alone. Eating a solitary meal or sneaking in to watch a film on your own seemed understandable: there was the gastronomic pleasure or psychological lift to balance the lack of company, but bowling was emotionally dangerous even if you were in a couple or with your family, let alone a single man.

Even if you had ten games in a row, you'd still want one more to get it right. Everything is waiting to let you down – the curve of the ball, the muscles in your back, the lace of your shoe. And it always leaves you tired and unsatisfied, waiting for the next time to rectify your mistakes.

The man sent his final ball down towards the three remaining pins. He stood there in his blue jeans and green shirt, crouching slightly as he waited for the ball to connect. Two pins shot back, but the third shrugged off the attack and remained upright. I watched the man as he sat down on a blue plastic chair and unlaced his bowling shoes. Then a customer blocked my view.

'Yes?' I said, trying to look over her shoulder.

'Sarah.'

She was smiling. I couldn't believe she was smiling. I've never understood why people think that not seeing someone for a while makes up for their past misdeeds. Adrian hovered behind me, sensing drama.

'Hello Lesley. How many games are you having?'

She laughed, and tried to touch me. Fortunately, there was a cash register between us. Her hair was lighter than ever, almost yellow. This surprised me. When I'd known her, she'd always been trying to darken it.

'Did Adrian tell you I'd visited?'

Typical Lesley. Getting everyone's name like a paranoid old lady. I'd have much more respect for her if she didn't try so hard. I stared at her.

'You alone?'

She nodded, biting her lip. 'Yes, but I need to talk to you about that. I need to talk to you about everything.'

'Where are you staying?'

'The Prince Regent. Do you know it?'

I nodded. 'I finish at midnight. Is that too late to come up?'

'No, that's fine.'

'Right. Should I come to your room?'

'If you like. It's number twelve.'

The Prince Regent was in the main bank of Sand Bay hotels, only five doors from Henry's rest home. I imagined him sleeping there as I walked up the hill, wondering if he felt the same anxiety that had driven me today when he was forced to stay in his room. When I reached Lesley's hotel, I peered through the thick-glass foyer doors, hoping the receptionist would be awake and prepared to let me in. He smiled and stood up, brushing his waistcoat as he came across.

He unlocked the door. 'Sarah Patton?'

'That's right.'

'Go on up. She's on the second floor.'

The only illumination in the room came from a fluorescent striplight above the sink. Lesley smiled at me.

'I'm sorry about this. The bulb's gone.'

'Where should I sit?'

'Have the chair. I'm happy to lie on the bed.'

I sat down. Lesley walked to her dressing table. I could make out a bottle and two glasses. 'You still drink Martini, don't you?'

I didn't answer.

'Pull back the curtains a bit. I can just about see with the lights outside.'

I did as she instructed. The Martini slopped audibly into each glass. She handed me one.

'I'm sorry I was funny in the bowling alley. I just know how much you hate making a fuss in public.'

'Does Charlie know you're here?'

'Of course. He was against it.'

'So why have you come? Is there a problem with Melissa?'

'No, she's fine. Don't you read Sandra's letters?'

'Do you?'

'Of course not. But I know she writes to you, and I know she's written about Melissa.'

I rubbed my shoe along the fringe of the rug. 'She's met a new man. A man who likes puppets.'

'So you do care.'

I ignored her taunt. She sat up and moved towards me, her voice rising. 'I know it was stupid to come here without telling you, okay? But you wouldn't keep running if you didn't think we'd come after you.'

I kept my voice even. 'I'm not running.'

'Okay, Sarah, I don't want to argue. I'm just fed up of feeling guilty.'

'It's not my fault if you feel guilty. I've never accused you of anything.'

'Then let's just resolve all this. There's no reason for us to be angry with each other. You've got your life . . .'

I couldn't resist. 'And you've got mine.'

She laughed, a bitter sound. 'You really still believe that, don't you? Do you think I like being the prop that supports your entire fucking family?'

I yawned. 'I'm too tired for this.'

'Sarah, please talk to me.'

'I'm sorry, I'm not going to sit here arguing in the dark. I'm tired and I've got work tomorrow.'

'Sleep here.'

'It doesn't feel right. When are you going?'

'Wednesday.'

'I'll meet you for dinner tomorrow night. But only to talk. I'm not going over all this again.'

'Okay. Where?'

'The Wayfarer. Eight o'clock.'

The receptionist smiled at me.

'I suppose you want letting out now.'

'If you wouldn't mind.'

He walked across the foyer and unlocked the door. 'Take care then. Night night.'

I took the quietest route back to Sylvia's, avoiding the centre. Talking to Lesley had left me light-headed, and I wondered if I sounded as unconvincing to her as I did to myself. One of my most successful self-deceptions has been believing that I've always determined everything that's happened to me. I would never have come to Weston if it wasn't for Lesley. Seeing her again made me realise that although I think of Charlie and Melissa all the time, Lesley never enters my mind. Talking to her tonight was like being confronted with an embarrassing part of my adolescence that I'd managed to forget but nevertheless influenced everything I'd done since. Lesley belonged to a time I didn't want to remember, and I felt eager to get back to my room at Sylvia's. I felt tempted to take another day off, but I knew the longer I stalled the less likely I'd be to return. And I needed my job. It was the one source of stability I had left.

5

Tuesday

Sitting behind a computer is the best way to hide tiredness. A blank face is easy to spot if it's staring into space, but if the weary eyes are directed at a dissolving screen, people will pass by without comment. That was my main reason for persuading Paul to get me a PC, even though our entire operation could be stored on one floppy disc. Most days I didn't bother turning it on, but this morning I needed a break.

When I felt hands on my shoulders, I assumed they belonged to Paul, and prayed the moving fingers weren't Neil's. But then I noticed purple nail varnish.

'How's it going?' asked Mary.

'Not bad. I'm a bit knackered.'

'Late night?' she asked, leaning down. Her pendant slipped beneath my top.

'Too late,' I told her.

'Neil?' she asked.

'No, it wasn't a man. A friend from home decided to drop in on me.'

'That's nice. We should go on a girls' night out together.'

'I don't know how long she's staying,' I lied.

'What about you and me then? We haven't gone out in a while.'

'How about Thursday?'

'Thursday, I think that's okay. I'll let you know.'

'Do you know what time Neil's due in?'

'No, he wasn't here yesterday. I thought you two were taking a sickie.'

I looked at Mary, thinking. That explained why Paul came round yesterday. 'You didn't say anything to Paul, did you?'

'Of course not. But I think he was a bit suspicious.'

'Oh God.'

'Relax. You weren't doing anything.'

She patted my shoulder and moved on. Irritated, I tapped the keys with the edge of my fingernails, measuring exactly how little effort was required to produce each letter. What excuse did Neil have for taking a day off? I closed my file and walked into Paul's office.

'Hello Sarah. Feeling better?' His voice sounded light, but he wasn't looking at me.

'Yes thanks. The doctor said I ought to take another day, but I was fed up of lying in bed.'

He looked up. 'You sure you're all right?'

'I hope so. I've downed a bottle of Pepto-Bismol so that should keep my stomach quiet. How did things go yesterday?'

'Okay. We didn't really get much done,' he said, watching me. 'You know Neil wasn't in either.'

'Yeah, Mary told me. What was wrong with him?'

'I don't know. Mary took the call. Probably the same thing you had. Have you two been eating in the same place?'

'I doubt it. Not on the weekend. We go to the same dodgy

sandwich shop, but I don't think it would've stayed in our systems that long. Is he back today?'

'I presume so. He hasn't called.'

He made the statement sound unfinished, as if waiting for me to complete it. I didn't want Paul to doubt me, even if I was being unfaithful to him. I'd always felt we trusted one another, and didn't like the idea of losing that. I remembered Paul's confused expression when he showed me his wife's diaries, and hated contributing to his suspicion of women.

He looked much smarter than usual today, and I wondered if Iona had been buying him new clothes. His blue shirt was too bright for him, the youthful cut making him look old. I wondered if he expected me to compliment him, and didn't just in case. I smiled at him and left the office.

Mary looked expectant.

'Everything okay?' she asked.

'Fine.'

Neil arrived at nine thirty. All my hopes that he'd be able to act gracefully looked futile. His jaw chewed even more languidly than usual, and he entered the office as Paul once had, striding positively into his domain. Mary grinned at him and he winked at her, making his way to my desk.

'I've missed you,' he said.

'Shsss,' I told him.

'What's wrong?'

'Just don't say that here.'

'Why not? Paul can't hear us.'

'I know, but we mustn't act like lovers. It'll be too easy to make a slip.'

'Okay,' he said, smiling, 'but don't accuse me of ignoring you.'

'I won't. Go tell Paul you're in.'

Neil frowned and walked through to Paul's office. I stared at my screen, uncertain how best to spin out the small tasks I'd set myself this morning. I considered redesigning the spreadsheets for the summer accounts. That sort of layout impressed Paul, and I wanted to please him. My fingers rotated the mouse, spiralling the cursor as I waited for Neil to return.

I heard Paul's laughter as Neil left the office. He walked back to my desk.

'He doesn't know anything. You worry too much.'

'Maybe,' I conceded, 'but try not to make it obvious.'

He stared at me, clearly irritated. I wished I could touch him.

'What are you doing tonight?' I asked.

'I don't know yet.'

My voice grew higher. 'Would you like to go out with me?'

'Maybe.'

'I'd really appreciate it. A friend from home has come to visit me. I think you'd like her.'

He stopped chewing. I'd expected this to catch his attention. I hoped he was intrigued because he wanted to find out about my background, but worried he might just want to meet another older woman. I felt angry at Neil for making me doubt him.

'Okay,' he said. 'Where and when?'

I arrived early, but Lesley was still waiting for me. I could tell from the number of cigarette butts that she'd been there for at least fifteen minutes, ensuring her resentment remained strong.

'Sorry I'm on time,' I told her, 'I should have realised you'd be early.'

Her handbag rested against the laminated menu. Lesley

was wearing a pink ribbed T-shirt and blue jeans. Her hair was held back with an Alice band. She looked suburban, but she liked to dress in character, and I suspected she'd chosen these clothes to mock me, showing that she too could pass here undetected.

'Staying up late with you really knocked me out,' I said, 'I've been no use to anyone all day.'

She stubbed out her cigarette. 'You have to preface everything, don't you?'

'I can't help it if I'm tired. I do have a job.'

Neil entered the restaurant. I smiled at him and he approached our table.

'Lesley, this is my boyfriend, Neil. I hope you don't mind him joining us, but I've told him so much about you, and he's eager to meet a friend of mine from home. It's okay, isn't it?'

I knew she wouldn't make a scene. 'Of course,' she said. She offered Neil her hand and he shook it, smiling at her. Neil slipped in next to me and the waiter approached with his pad.

'Ready to order?'

'Lesley?'

She nodded, and asked for chicken and chips and a cup of tea. Neil and I both ordered fish. He was wearing the same white shirt and grey trousers he'd worn to work. I felt glad he'd left the jacket at home. Lesley stared at me. I smiled at her, pleased that I was finally getting my turn to orchestrate things.

Lesley began by looking bored whenever a question was directed at her. Once she realised this strategy was amusing me, she attempted to flirt with Neil, starting by asking him about me. Neil's tale sounded surprisingly genuine, and I wondered why I'd doubted his sincerity. He told her how he'd had lots of offers of proper work with other companies. Insurance agencies, solicitors, computer manufacturers. Jobs that would stretch his mind and provide useful contacts for the future. But none of these offers had excited him as much as his five-minute interview with me. He described how disappointed he'd felt when he came to Weston and realised I wasn't available. And then his slow discovery that he might have a chance, after all. How he'd asked Mary to lay the groundwork, describing her as the good fairy who'd brought us together. He let her know our love had been consummated, while remaining discreet about the details. Then he took my hand, and told Lesley he'd never felt happier.

I've spent many hours working out exactly what attracts men to Lesley. Her approach is simple, and effective. She is naturally self-deprecating, and uses this to her advantage. As soon as she meets a man she lets him know she doesn't expect to be found attractive, immediately pointing out any better-looking women in her company. But once she's set herself up as unlovable, she hints that her self-knowledge means that she's prepared to do anything to please her man. Consequently, even men who see no value in Lesley are forced to acknowledge her, because not to do so is to join the other ordinary men who have already passed her by. Somehow Neil remained immune to all this, and when she invited unfavourable comparisons between her beauty and mine, he simply agreed with her. I hadn't expected this commitment, and felt a flush of happy pride.

Neil excused himself and walked to the toilet. Lesley leaned across the table and said to me: 'I can see this is fun for you.'

I lifted my fork to my mouth. 'Aren't you enjoying yourself?'

'Sarah, your mum told me to come here. If I go back and

tell her how you've treated me, she'll be up here within the hour.'

'No she won't. She knows what'll happen if she looks for me.'

'Why are you being so difficult?'

'Why aren't you happy for me? I've got a good job, two good jobs, a boyfriend who loves me.'

'You work in a bowling alley and you're going out with an adolescent. Your mother would be disgusted.'

Her nastiness proved she was jealous of me, and I wasn't going to be upset by her taunts. I'm sure Lesley wanted to find me lying in a gutter, just so she'd have the satisfaction of being the one who rehabilitated me. The only time I'd called my father since arriving in Weston, he'd told me that he'd dreamt he got a phonecall from someone claiming to be a friend of mine, asking him to come here immediately. When he reached Weston the friend told him that as soon as I heard he was coming I ran away. When they found me I was wearing a shiny black latex suit with my hair gelled into a vicious point. As they approached, I flopped onto the ground, and every time they tried to lift me, I kept slipping out of their grasp. Not knowing what to do, they tried to carry me to a hospital, but with every few steps I slipped away again, crashing to the ground with increasingly damaging force.

'Why don't you come home for a couple of days?' she asked, softening her voice. 'Melissa's birthday's coming up . . .'

'I know.'

'Then perhaps this year you'll send her a card.'

Neil returned from the toilet. After the comment about his age, Lesley couldn't continue flirting with Neil, and her silence allowed us to swap flippant banter and talk about work.

'Where next?' Neil asked.

'I'm leaving tomorrow,' said Lesley, 'so I ought to go home and pack.'

'What time are you going?' I asked.

'Around two. I don't have to be back until evening.'

'Let's meet in the morning then. I'll come round before work.'

She stared at me, her expression exaggeratedly weary. 'Only if you feel up to it. Nice to meet you, Neil.'

'Likewise,' he said.

We walked past the Cascade and Mr B's Fun Factory. I watched a child riding on a miniature big wheel, shrieking with laughter as he rose into the air. As soon as Lesley had gone, I embraced Neil and kissed him hard.

'Thank you,' I told him.

'What for?' he asked.

'Being you. Being brilliant.'

'Do you think she liked me then?'

'She called you an adolescent.'

'Oh.'

'No, that's brilliant. It shows she can't cope with the idea of me being with you. Neil, I'm so grateful for tonight.'

He smiled. I had an idea. Taking his arm, I said: 'Remember when you told me about your beach fantasy? I didn't tell you then because I didn't know if I could trust you, but the thing is I've always been scared of doing something like that, but if I was with you I think I might enjoy it.'

He grinned. 'Yeah?'

'Only it has to be exactly as you imagined it. It's too light to go down to the beach yet, so what I thought was we could buy a bottle and go back to my place. Then you could choose what you'd like me to wear from my wardrobe. I could wear the clothes you liked from the Clevedon trip if you want.'

'Oh Sarah,' he said, 'that would be wonderful.'

Neil seemed overwhelmed by my enthusiasm, not understanding how long I've waited to let myself go. Before now, I had limited my actions with him so he wouldn't demand more than I could give, taking his arm or touching his hand only when I thought he would understand the significance of the gesture. Now I was leaning my whole body against him, my arm slung low around his buttocks, with my hand thrust deep into his back pocket. At school we called girls who did this 'goalkeepers', because they looked like they were trying to hold two footballs at once.

Once we'd reached Sylvia's we raced upstairs and I pushed Neil onto the mattress. Opening my wardrobe, I pulled out a handful of dresses, skirts and shirts, and spread them on the bed.

'So,' I said, 'what do you want to see me in?'

'What's beneath the plastic cover?' he asked, pointing to the dress hooked to the back of the door.

'Close your eyes,' I said, slipping my blue PVC dress from its protective sleeve.

I smoothed the dress over my flawed skin and told Neil to hang on while I gelled my hair and applied make-up. I turned out the main light and swivelled the bedside lamp to make it look as if I was standing on a stage.

'You look beautiful,' he said, 'but you can't wear that down to the beach. The sand will ruin it.'

'I don't care,' I told him. 'The dress was designed for a special occasion, and I can't think of anything more special than being with you.'

We drank. It got dark. I didn't want Neil to think my excitement had waned so I left my glass half finished and took his hand. We walked to the Sea Front, striding as quickly as we could without beginning to jog.

The necklace man stood in his normal nightly position, but I refused to be intimidated by my memories. Tonight would be unique. I kept smiling at Neil, my hand still squeezing his behind. We jumped down onto the sand.

'Where do you want to do it?' I asked.

'Beneath the pier. It's darker there.'

'Neil,' I began, 'if there's other people there, it won't put you off, will it?'

He spoke to me as if addressing an expert. 'Will there be other people there?'

'I don't know. I came here once, a long time ago. There were people there then.'

He looked at me. 'It doesn't matter,' he said. 'In the dark, it'll seem like we're alone.'

I grabbed his hand and pulled him onwards. Under the pier, I dropped to my knees and crawled away from him. He pushed his weight down onto my back, squashing me into the wet sand. The PVC gripped my body as he pulled the dress up around my waist, making me feel like a beached mermaid. He stroked my inner thighs, his dry, soft hand a pleasant contrast to the grit on my neck and face. Before long, our wrestling became lovemaking and in spite of all my fears, I thought not of Sandy Bay and losing my virginity, but of my sister dropping coins through the pier slats. Only in my imagination, she was no longer dropping coins but instead little golden raindrops that melted into Neil's back, bled into me through his prick, and burned my eyes when I came.

Wednesday

It was worth waking early to get Lesley out of my life. The receptionist recognised me and made a joke about how I always disturbed his rest. I walked up to the second floor. Lesley had left the door open and sat wrapped in three hotel towels. I handed her an envelope.

'Can you give this to Melissa? For her birthday.'

Lesley took the card and looked at me. I couldn't tell if she was surprised or suspicious.

'There's money inside so I don't want to post it. Tell her how much I miss her.'

'Okay,' she said, 'any message for Sandra?'

'Yeah. Tell Mum I've got her letters and I'll write as soon as I get a chance.'

She nodded. 'It ought to be soon though, Sarah. She's getting herself into a real state.'

'It will be.'

Lesley stretched her arm towards me. 'Come in and sit down. I'm not going anywhere until I've got dressed.'

I sat by the window. She stood up.

'Close that curtain, will you? I don't want to give some pervert a peep show.'

I did as she instructed. Lesley uncoiled the towel from her head and combed the hair from her eyes. Her suitcase lay on the bed. She'd left a black dress hanging on the front of the wardrobe. Her socks and underwear sat in small balls on the mattress. The suitcase wobbled as she pulled her socks on and slipped her knickers up under the second towel. Then she unwrapped both towels and stood up. I didn't want her to think she was embarrassing me so I held her gaze, then looked down to her body. She seemed thinner than I remembered, and had two dark creases running across her stomach.

'I'm sorry about last night,' I said, feeling generous. 'I didn't mean to make you feel awkward.'

She exhaled. 'That's okay. I shouldn't have said that stuff about Neil.'

I looked at her breasts, remembering how envious I used to feel towards girls with normal nipples. I wondered if Charlie had ever talked to her about my body. Then I asked: 'What did you think of him, Lesley? Seriously?'

'Neil?' I waited while she fastened her bra. 'He looks like that bloke from the park. The one you made me kiss.'

'Really? I don't remember.'

'My first snog and I didn't get his name. You got me in so much trouble.'

'You remember it wrong. I was the one who got in trouble. Your dad said I'd corrupted you.'

'Your mum didn't care. She laughed about it afterwards.'

'Afterwards, maybe, but she was furious at the time. She was terrified of your parents. She thought they were going to burn her as a witch.'

Lesley laughed. 'I loved coming to your house, Sarah. I never imagined it was possible for families to get along like that.'

'Yes. Well.'

I felt my lips tighten. I unfolded my arms and tried not

to be churlish. Lesley took the dress from the hanger, bunching it up before slipping it over her head. She checked her reflection.

'How's Charlie?' I asked.

She looked at me. 'He still calls me Sarah sometimes.'

'When he's going to sleep, when he's just dropping off, does he sometimes shake himself awake?'

Lesley nodded. 'I asked him about it.'

'What did he say?'

'He said it was nothing and got all upset. I thought it was to do with you.'

'He was doing it before he met me. I think something terrible happened to him in his past. I just wondered if he'd told you what it was.'

'He wouldn't tell me something he hadn't told you. You're still the love of his life.'

'What does he say about me?'

'He says he couldn't live up to your expectations. I was the easy option.'

I looked at her. 'You do still love him, don't you?'

'Of course.'

'Look after him, Lesley. He's not as strong as he seems.'

'I know.'

Her quiet reply made me realise how patronising I sounded. I had a horrible recollection of the way I used to treat her, making her sit on my bed while I lectured her about love. She stepped into her shoes, straightening the heel with her finger. It was time for me to go.

'Can't you give me something to take back, Sarah? What if Sandra called you? Would you answer?'

I took a pen from the dressing table and wrote my number on a serviette. I handed it to Lesley. She nodded and folded the tissue into her purse.

'Okay?' I asked.

'Okay.'

Sylvia had been very grudging about letting me use her kitchen. I understood her reluctance, knowing this room was one of the few private spaces in the guest house. Nevertheless, I still felt disappointed to have discovered the limits of her generosity so quickly, especially as I wouldn't be going into the kitchen until well after the evening meal, by which time she'd be happily ensconced in the TV room.

At lunchtime, I went across to the Dolphin Bowl. After my troubles with Sylvia, I thought I wouldn't be able to get out of work, but Adrian said he'd find a girl to do my shift for me. The way he said 'a girl' made me think he'd met someone, but I couldn't imagine anyone sleeping with Adrian, not even a woman his equal in weight and looks. I could tell he wanted to ask why I wasn't coming to work, and knew he connected my request to Lesley's appearance on Monday evening, so I tried to keep my explanations cryptic, thinking that now I had Neil I'd probably need lots more nights off.

Walking back to March Entertainments, I began to feel guilty about the way I'd been dodging work commitments lately. It was as if I had Henry's money already, and although I knew it was unlikely he'd withdraw the offer I didn't like the way I'd started relying on imaginary cash. I wondered if Henry had known how just making the offer would change my life, and decided he must do. After all, he was the veteran of enough financial relationships to understand the power of even the most good-natured contracts.

Mary came with me to the supermarket after work, promising she'd help me prepare a delicious meal. She'd gained an idea of my culinary ineptitude on the night of the dinner party, but still claimed she could find something easy to cook that Neil would like.

Sorting out Lesley had filled me with physical confidence. I vowed to cut down my drinking and start eating decent food. I'd give up cigarettes for good and get more exercise. Use primrose oil instead of dark chocolate. Keep my skin clean and sign up for an anonymous AIDS test. Tomorrow I'd go to a sportshop and buy a new tracksuit and some trainers.

'He likes chicken, doesn't he?'

'Yeah, but you did chicken for the dinner party. I want to cook something he wouldn't normally have.'

'Something exotic? Seafood's good. Squid, or mussels maybe?' She giggled. 'How about oysters?'

I looked at her. 'We don't need any help in that department.'

'What about steak? Men are always impressed by a woman who'll cook steak for them.'

'Does Neil like steak?'

'I'm sure he does.'

'Isn't it a bit plain.'

'Do a sauce to go with it. Barbecue's easy. You'll need some brown sugar . . .'

She pushed the trolley away from me. I followed behind, listening as she selected ingredients and explained what to do with them. She sounded so earnest, and I marvelled that I'd found a friend who was that concerned about my love life. Mary seemed genuinely eager that my evening passed successfully, and I rubbed her shoulder to let her know how much her help meant to me. She smiled back, apologising for getting carried away.

'That's okay,' I told her, 'you're making me feel confident. I only wish I could help you with Ben.'

She laughed. 'I'll hold you to that.'

Neil arrived thirty minutes late. Rare steak became well done. I acted unconcerned, knowing how stupid it'd be to lay into him. But I felt insulted, and couldn't believe his grubby clothes. I know I'd always been dubious about his suits, but tonight he was wearing *red jeans*. It was at least two years since I'd seen someone in coloured denim, and his pair had been washed so often they were almost pink. Equally as unforgivable was his grey T-shirt, the type they used to give away free at Concept Man.

'No starter, I'm afraid,' I told Neil as I put his plate down in front of him, 'but there's plenty of wine.'

'Looks like you've started on it already,' he said, looking at the half-empty bottle of white.

'I've got red for the meal. Red goes better with steak.'

I started working at the bottle with the corkscrew, pulling his glass into reach. I poured two large measures, hoping the drink would remove the combative energies I sensed between us.

'It's a barbecue sauce,' I told him, 'Mary helped me.'

He cut a long sliver of steak and lifted it to his mouth. 'It's nice,' he said, chewing slowly. 'The meat's a little tough.'

'Sorry,' I said, looking down at my own plate. 'I wasn't sure when you'd be coming round.'

He offered no explanation or apology, instead drinking deep from his glass. 'Thanks for making me food, Sarah. I don't often get to eat properly.'

'It's hard, isn't it, when you live alone. Sylvia cooks most of my meals, but if I miss dinner I don't bother doing it for myself.'

He nodded. I cut myself a slice of steak, curious how my barbecue sauce had turned out. It tasted nice soaked into the meat, but the additional cooking time had caused the glazing to blacken into flavourless crisps. Still, I felt pleased with my new skill, and looked forward to startling Paul by offering to cook for him. The mange-tout had suffered less from Neil's tardiness, and the carrots' tasty crunch was a pleasant change from the mushy orange mess Sylvia served up. Only the wine tasted wrong, the flavour too blackcurranty to go well with the steak. And that was hardly my fault.

'I've thought about last night all day,' I told Neil. 'Was it everything you expected?'

He nodded. 'It was nice.'

'Did you really think all those things about me?'

'What things?'

'The things you told Lesley. About why you came here.'

'Of course.'

'Nobody's ever said stuff like that about me.'

He looked up. 'So what about you? What did you think about me?'

'You seemed strong,' I said.

'Strong in what way?'

'Ambitious. Like Paul, but different.'

'Like Paul?'

'A little bit. But I can see you're going to be much more successful. You don't have that shroud of failure that Paul has. But there's that same fighting instinct in your eyes.'

I refilled his glass. He leaned his chair back. 'I'm not really like that. Well, I am, but the ambitious part is only one side of me. I've got lots of other qualities.'

'I know,' I said, smiling at him.

'I'm not sure you do.'

'What makes you say that?'

'You're different to me. Your whole life is designed so that it can be thrown away at any minute. I take things a little more seriously.'

'I don't feel that way about you,' I protested.

'Not yet.'

He reached for the bottle and poured himself another glass, as if getting ready for my reply. I knew he expected me to argue back, but couldn't tell if his words came from insecurity or a desire to belittle me. Or both. I was already familiar with Neil's aggressive approach to romance, and knew silence was the worst response. But I'd had such high expectations for tonight that I couldn't bring myself to say anything, sadly fingering the bottom of my black velvet dress and wondering if it was still sunny outside.

'Don't be angry because I see through you, Sarah. You know you'd despise me if I didn't question you. You can resist being normal for ever, but I know you don't want to be stuck in Weston when you're forty.'

I stroked the stem of my glass, knowing he was trying to guide my reply. Why was no one prepared to believe I might be serious about my life? Even Neil, almost ten years younger than me, thought he could understand every choice I'd ever made after a handful of dates.

'I like my life, Neil. I came here because I wanted to be free.'

'You're not free,' he snapped, his voice rising. 'You work in a cardboard office intimidating people into believing you're providing a useful service. You spend three nights a week giving shoes to fat, smelly families who think chucking a ball down a strip of polished wood constitutes exercise. And when you're not working you're getting fucked by a balding, middle-aged man who treats you like a slag.'

My response was automatic. 'So you think I'm a slag?'

'I didn't say that. All I know is that you must be fucking cold to get everything you need from your lifestyle.'

'Fine,' I said, 'so I'm cold again. What a surprise. Neil, do you think these are original observations? I'm surrounded by people who tell me I'm cold and call me a bitch, and if that's true, why don't you all fuck off and leave me alone?'

He looked at me. I was trembling. He had his emotional reaction. As I expected, he put his arms around me and said in a soothing voice, 'Okay, I'm sorry, I went too far. Forgive me.'

He was brimming with adolescent enthusiasm, his hard

penis pressing against me as he made a show of being apologetic. I shoved him away. He backed into the table, knocking the bottle off. It hit the floor without breaking, spilling wine onto the carpet. Neither of us made any attempt to right it.

'You're an arrogant prick,' I told him, 'you know that.'

He tried not to smile. I wanted to throw him out, but I couldn't help it: his attack had aroused me and I wanted to fuck a sincere apology out of him. My reaction to his boldness made me wonder what would happen if I treated Henry and Paul with similarly youthful disdain. Somehow I doubted they'd be so enthusiastic. I led Neil to the bed and pushed him face down into the mattress, vowing to keep him prisoner at least until I'd made him cry.

5

Thursday

The worst thing about only having one room is that I'm always faced with evidence of what happened the night before. Sylvia would be in after breakfast and quite apart from the dirty plates and ransacked bed, there was the less easily resolvable problem of the wine-soaked carpet. But first I needed to know how much time I had.

I searched for five minutes before noticing the grey plastic square in Neil's hand. Even then I was reluctant to give up my conviction that the sun had woken me early, and wondered why Neil had fallen asleep clutching my clock instead of acknowledging that the alarm had sounded and been silenced, allowing us to sleep on until, *until* . . . I looked at the clock . . . *ten twenty*. I shook Neil awake.

'We're late.'

'So? Call in sick.'

'Not again. Paul'll never believe we've been ill on the same day twice. You take the day off and I'll go in. I'll say I organised a meeting and forgot to tell him. Please Neil, even if you do think my life is meaningless, don't fuck it up for me.'

He lifted his face from the pillow. 'I'm not like that, Sarah.'

I looked at his ruffled hair and then around to the room. 'I know it's a lot to ask, but if you are staying here this morning, could you straighten the place a bit? My landlady's old.'

'No problem,' he said. 'Say hi to Paul and Mary.'

I told Paul I'd been up to Brighter Futures, looking into how a promotions company could enliven the rest home's social programme. Mentioning Henry's place of residence served as a good red herring, not denying Paul his jealousy but redirecting it towards a safer target. Consequently, he felt both justified and relieved, asking me if I knew where Neil was without a trace of suspicion.

'No idea.'

'He can't be ill again already. He's given up bothering.'

'We did say this might happen. It's not as if we've got a lot to offer him.'

'Maybe, but Mary's just as good and she still turns up. I don't suppose you want to talk to him?'

'I will if you want, but he'll take it more seriously coming from you.'

'Perhaps I should just get rid of him. I'm sure his wages could be better spent elsewhere.'

He looked at me. I shrugged.

'I won't do anything for the minute, but if he carries on taking the piss . . .'

'Fair enough,' I agreed, 'he's had enough chances.'

Mary immediately called me over to her desk. She grinned.

'I take it dinner went well then. Or is this another coincidence?'

'I left him tidying up,' I giggled. 'Are you still on for tonight?'

'Of course. Meet by the Grand Central again?'
'Good idea.'

I spent the afternoon with Henry. We went to The Wayfarer and then walked down to the beach. We fed the seagulls and avoided talking about the obvious change in our relationship. Sitting there with him, eating ice cream and laughing, I wondered if once I stopped feeling rejected, I might come to enjoy these afternoons as much as I had liked going to bed with him. He was much more friendly to me than he'd been before, and there was none of the stress that had recently come between us. It occurred to me that going to bed with Henry had been a way of legitimising our relationship, and that in my mind it seemed more perverse to be Henry's friend than his lover. We parted friends, and he mentioned that he might pop round on Sunday after all.

I went home expecting the worst. I couldn't decide whether he was more likely to have forgotten about tidying up and gone home, or to still be there waiting for me to help him. My suspicions seemed confirmed when I noticed Sylvia waiting for me.

'I'm sorry, Sylvia,' I began, 'I didn't mean to leave the room like that.'

'It was fine when I went in,' she said, 'and complete with a charming stranger.'

I smiled. 'Did you like him?'

'Very much. And you must do too if you're cooking him dinner. I never thought I'd see you doing that for a man.' She looked at me. 'I hope that doesn't sound awful.'

'No, not at all. I'd never have cooked for Henry, but it seemed different with Neil.'

'Young men are lovely, aren't they? Especially boyish ones

like Neil. I've never understood why you haven't gone after men your own age.'

'He's ten years younger than me.'

'Really? I'm hopeless at judging ages. That makes you the older woman. I bet that feels strange.'

'We haven't been together long. But I like it so far.'

'I'm glad. It's so nice to see you happy, Sarah. You haven't had things easy.'

Her face glowed with indulgent approval, her eyes and smile exuding a lazy, accepting love that made me feel inadequate. I wanted to reply with my usual disclaimer, the same mantra I'd repeated to Neil and Lesley when they showed concern for me. *I chose this life. You have no reason to pity me.* But at the same time, the child in me wanted to crawl into her lap and start crying, explaining how the knowledge that I'd made such an effort to shape my life like this made the bleak times even harder to live through.

'Will we see you for dinner tonight?' she asked.

I nodded.

My room wasn't spotless. A kidney-shaped shadow marked the spot where the wine had spilt, and the dirty tablecloth had been left hanging over the back of two chairs. But he'd made the place smart enough for Sylvia, and that was all I had asked. He'd even left a note on the pillow, written in biro on a torn piece of newspaper:

Sarah,

I'm sorry about being horrible. I hope you'll let me make it up to you. Talk to you soon,

Love,

Neil

I pulled back my duvet and buried my face into the sheets,

hoping my boy had left his scent behind. The odour of teenager was disappointingly faint, but I consoled myself with a resolution to buy a canister of Lynx when I went shopping on Saturday. I read the note again, surprised, after last night, by its lightness. I sensed I had more to learn about Neil, and thought that Sylvia had forgotten the most exciting aspect of dating someone young: the sense of discovery. It'd only taken a couple of nights to understand Paul. Maybe a fortnight with Henry. But Neil probably didn't even understand himself yet, and I'd get to witness years of changes before he decided on the personality he wanted to keep.

Being upstaged by Mary no longer worried me, and I changed clothes only so she wouldn't think I was dirty. I picked out an old pink shirt that I'd bought years ago as something smart and now only wore with jeans. I was looking forward to going out with Mary, mainly because I knew she wouldn't mind me going on about Neil, and boring her seemed healthier than reliving last night alone. I knew a time would come when I'd want to examine my relationship in solitude, but for the moment being in love seemed like a good reason to do all the things I usually avoided.

The evening meal was one of Sylvia's pick 'n' mix specials: pizza slice, sausage rolls, vol-au-vents. Sylvia saved dishes like this for the hotter nights, not wanting to waste effort on food destined to be pushed to the side of the plate. I ate the pizza and left the rest, saving myself for two portions of ice cream.

I could only manage half an hour in the TV room, setting off at the end of the news. I anticipated a long wait beneath the Grand Central clock, but Mary'd also come out early. She patted my arms and kissed me, the second gesture making me twist awkwardly.

She raised her eyebrows. 'The Princess?'

'Of course.'

I followed Mary as she walked back through the arcade-lined streets. The usual crowds of teenagers stood staring out of each entrance, defiantly eyeing up their doubles on the opposite side of the road. Their grim resolution made them look like sailors in rival galleons, travelling in parallel lines. A drunk in his mid-twenties staggered down the road towards us. He was wearing an old-fashioned red tracksuit, with two white stripes running down the arms and legs. The tracksuit had been stretched out of its proper proportions and made his limbs seem dangerously spindly, as if on the verge of snapping. I touched Mary's arm, telling her to cross the road. Instead she laughed and shouted: 'Jim.'

The man's unsteady head bobbed back up and I recognised Neil's friend from The Star, the man who'd eaten glass for a bet. He smiled at us. I wondered if he remembered me. Mary strode across, halting his path with her palm.

'I thought you were in Spain.'

'Nah,' he said, eyes directed away from her, 'I couldn't go.'

'How come?'

'I hadn't really got the time off work. I was planning to blag it, but then I got a bad appraisal.'

'What did they say?'

Jim continued staring into the arcade. A layer of clear, crusted mucus glistened across his ratty moustache. Mary repeated her question.

He swallowed. 'My supervisor called me into her office and said she'd heard reports that I'd been drinking and taking drugs on the way to work. And that morning I'd been doing your speed, see, so she could see it in my eyes.' He shook his head. 'But I told her she was talking rubbish, so she got all official and said, "Well, in that case, Jim, how do *you* think this month's gone?" So I says, 'Well, first you had Lucky Lady at 7–1 on and that didn't come in. Then you had Mary's Boy Child at 11–1 and didn't come in, and Monkey Magic was a fucking non-starter. So, basically, Miss, you owe me two dozen eggs.'

I laughed. Jim turned his gaze on me. He stared at me in silence. I wondered if he was trying to place my face. Then his lips curled into an expression of terrible pain.

'My teeth hurt so bad, Mary. If I get some pliers, could you pull them out?'

'I don't think that's a good idea, Jim.'

'Why not? I can get some more. There's a bloke at work who went through a windscreen and he got new teeth.'

He looked hopefully at Mary. When he realised she wouldn't be persuaded, he shrugged and said: 'Ah, well, see you then.'

He shuffled past us. I couldn't help laughing. Jim stopped, and walked back to me. He leaned in close. His breath made me feel sick.

'Are you made of wood?'

I didn't answer.

'It's a simple question. Either you is or you isn't. If you isn't, fair play. If you is . . .' He produced a purple lighter. '. . . then I'm gonna have to burn you.'

He flicked the flint and lifted the flame up beneath my nose. I knew he'd burn me if I didn't say anything, but I couldn't get the words out.

'No,' said Mary, 'she isn't made of wood.'

Jim nodded. 'That's all right then.'

He pocketed the lighter and walked off.

Mary told me to sit down while she fetched the drinks. Jim's inanity had left me trembling. I kept touching my nose, remembering the heat beneath it. I pictured the tip burnt black, then thought of Pinocchio. I wondered if memories of the puppet boy had inspired Jim's ramblings, then felt angry at myself for trying to rationalise the attack. Mary placed a Tia Maria in front of me.

'It's a double,' she said, 'for the shock.'

'Thank you.'

'I'm sorry. I shouldn't have called him over.'

'It wasn't your fault.'

'Maybe, but I'm sorry it happened.'

She looked away. I examined her intent features, wondering why she felt responsible. Then I remembered our walk along the pier, when she told me her new criteria for selecting sexual partners.

'Mary, Jim wasn't one of your unsuitable men, was he?'

She sighed. 'I didn't sleep with Jim.'

'What then?'

'Remember when we went to Clevedon and I told you I'd gone to a party in Bath with two blokes . . .'

'And it turned into an orgy so you walked out.'

'Sarah,' she said, starting to cry, 'I didn't walk out. And one of the blokes was Jim.'

I stroked her hand. 'It's okay.'

'I felt so disgusting. I thought I'd never be able to sleep with a man again. That's why I kept going to bed with you instead of Ben.'

She was really crying now, the force of her sobs embarrassing me. I sipped my drink, hoping the music was loud enough to keep her misery as private as possible. She kept staring at me as the tears ran down her face, as if she was offering her distress as a gift. I touched her hand again, wishing I wasn't so useless at providing comfort.

'Tell me the truth. What is it *exactly* that upsets you about that night?'

'It's everything,' she said, unhelpfully, 'I was drunk. I don't know what I did. I might have a disease.'

'Ah.'

'I'm not sure. I don't think that much happened *inside* of me, but I'm still scared.'

'Do you want to get a test? I could take you. I was planning to go myself.'

She shook her head. 'It's not just that, and anyway, I don't think I'd want to know. I've let everyone down.'

'Don't be stupid. You told me you came here because you were fed up of other people's expectations. All you're suffering from now is a bit of misplaced guilt. It goes away. I know you can't see it now, but later on you'll be glad of the bad times. You'll probably even brag about that party to a boyfriend who'll love you for your mysterious past.'

'You don't understand. I'm hurting people.'

'Sex can't hurt anyone. You're placing too much importance on a few indiscretions.'

'I'm so ashamed,' she sobbed.

'Why?'

'I can't tell you. I feel so sick of myself.'

'I'm not easily shocked,' I told her, my words light but truthful. I felt a prurient curiosity to know what Mary considered unsuitable for my ears. I waited, but she seemed to have completed her confession, maybe because she sensed it was being received with something other than sympathy. Being shut out at this point made me angry, even though I hadn't wanted to hear her sob story in the first place. I excused myself and went to the toilet, wanting a break before we changed topic.

'I'm sorry, Sarah,' she said as I returned, 'I really don't feel up to this.'

'Okay.'

'I wish I hadn't ruined your evening.'

'You didn't. Jim did.'

She laughed sadly. 'Let's go out next week. We'll catch a train and get out of Weston.'

'I'd like that.'

I finished my drink and we left the club. I walked back with her as far as the Odeon, then said goodnight. She kissed me again, and left me alone. I walked home quickly, seeing a red tracksuit in every shadowed corner.

5

Friday

Mary handed me a small bundle of violets. Their snipped stems were wrapped with blue paper, the soggy end dripping water onto my desk. Neither Paul nor Henry had ever bought me flowers, tactfully sensing how I'd respond to such a gesture. I thanked Mary, and asked if I should put them in water.

'I wouldn't worry,' she told me, 'you don't want dying flowers in your room. I shan't be offended if you throw them away.'

'I'll put them in that old jug. It'll be nice to have a bit of brightness on my desk.'

I fetched the brown china jug and took it to the small closet we used as both a kitchen and a toilet. Mary followed me.

'I wanted to thank you for last night. I didn't realise how much I needed to talk. When I got home I felt less stressed than I had in ages.'

I carried the jug back to my desk. 'I'll probably knock it over the computer and give myself an electric shock.'

'Yeah. Be careful.'

She returned to her desk. I continued typing, not noticing Paul come up behind me.

'Secret admirer?'

'Mary bought them. They're nice, aren't they?'

He didn't say anything, looking across the room to Mary. His fingers rested upon my shoulders, and he stared down at my screen. He murmured to himself, then walked away. I turned to watch him as he entered his office, realising that no matter how strong my love for Neil had become, I still felt a sad, stupid affection for my boss.

I didn't mean to argue with Neil. I'd planned to flatter him, explaining that I knew he was right and that it *was* stupid to carry on working in jobs that meant nothing to me, but that it'd take time for me to give up my old life, and as much as I wanted to spend Friday night with him, he'd have to meet me at midnight after the end of my shift. But when we started talking I became belligerent, responding to everything he said as if it were a personal attack. I hadn't even thanked him for tidying my room, or told him what a good impression he'd made on Sylvia. As we parted he agreed to meet me, but said he couldn't guarantee what state he'd be in. After all, he said, if you're going to waste tonight in a bowling alley, you can't complain if I spend it drinking with friends. Eager to end our bickering, I told him I'd be happy to see him no matter how many drinks he'd had.

It wasn't until I got to work that I wondered whether the friends Neil was drinking with would include Jim. As far as I was aware, Jim was one of the only friends Neil had in Weston. I knew how difficult it was to get to know people over the summer, but I couldn't imagine anyone relying on Jim for human contact. How could Neil know about the abscess rotting away in Jim's jaw and still look forward to sharing a drink with him? It was beyond my comprehension.

Adrian arrived thirty minutes into my shift, just before the start of the evening rush. His beard had gone. The newly revealed skin looked pink and tender, like recently healed scar tissue. Without his facial hair, Adrian looked much less foreboding. He still had a lumpy body and persisted in wearing his silly heavy metal rings and necklace, but he definitely seemed to have begun his return to normal society.

'What happened?' I asked.

He folded his leather jacket into an empty shoe shelf and turned to me, rubbing his smooth chin.

'I haven't got used to it yet. It feels weird.'

'How long have you had a beard?'

'Since I could grow one. A proper one, that is, not just bumfluff.'

He was still proud of it, I realised, even now it was gone. Adrian seemed such a curious man, so conceited, but happy to conceal his charms. I wondered if there were women out there who'd love him for his self-assurance. I also wondered, not for the first time, what he thought of me.

A young family were waiting. The mother paid for three frames, shifting her baby from one arm to the other as she took the money from her purse. The baby started at me, its pink tongue blobbing over its bottom lip.

'Lane nine,' I told them, 'the empty one in the middle.'

Adrian let me leave five minutes early and I went down to wait in the Square. It was colder than it'd been for a while, and I felt glad I'd brought my jacket. I was nervous about seeing Neil drunk, worried he'd be in an argumentative mood again. All I wanted tonight was cuddles and reassurance, and maybe some slow, gentle sex.

At least if he was drunk, he wouldn't be able to complain about my sweaty uniform. I'd have a shower as soon as we got back, but I was feeling a bit insecure and didn't want to give him any reason to recoil from me. I stared at myself in a shop window, using my comb to straighten my hair. I didn't think I looked too bad, and I'd tried to avoid the more physical jobs all evening.

I pushed my hand into the back of my trousers, pretending to tuck in my shirt but really wiping a line of sweat from around the cleft of my bottom, raising my fingers to my nose and humbling myself with the smell. I wondered which direction Neil would come from, thinking that he'd probably spent the night in The Star.

I looked at my wrist, then remembered leaving my watch at home. I should've stayed in the alley longer. I could've told Adrian I'd do the closing-up jobs, and come down around ten past twelve when Neil was bound to be here. I just had this silly conviction that he'd be early tonight.

I stood up and walked down to the bottom of the Square, hoping I'd see him staggering up. Someone was singing in another street, the voice loud and male. I had a sudden worry that Neil would turn up with Jim and all his other weird friends. It seemed the sort of thing he'd do to test me, and I told myself that if he did, I wouldn't complain. Our battle of egos proved this was a real relationship, and that we both felt it important to establish some ground rules.

I watched a drunk kick a Surprise Every Time machine, rattling the plastic chicken but failing to knock her from her perch. I wondered what the artificial bird had done to cause his displeasure. Probably taken his fifty pence and failed to produce a magic egg, seeing as the machine was switched off. The drunk's anger depressed me, and I walked back to my bench.

Adrian opened the side door of the alley and lifted his racing bike onto the paving stones. As far as I knew, this was at least his third bike, possibly his fourth. It'd taken him that many losses to persuade the alley managers to let him store his bike at the bottom of the stairwell, in the old cubicle that had once been used to hand out tickets. He straddled his bike and walked it slowly into the light, before curving round onto the road. I watched him pedal away, and realised that I felt a lot more nervous sitting here now he'd gone.

His departure meant it was at least ten past twelve, probably later given Adrian's thoroughness. I could lock myself into the alley, but then I wouldn't be able to see Neil arrive. The pubs were long closed now, and even if he'd stopped off to get chips, he ought to be here.

I wasn't going to wait any longer. He knew where I lived. I started walking back along the Square. But as I walked I pictured myself lying awake full of longing for him, unable to sleep for worry that his drunken shouts would wake Sylvia's guests and make her cross with me.

I hated this. This was the reason I'd stopped dating younger men. This was why I had such formal arrangements with Paul and Henry.

Paul.

I stopped by the phonebox, remembering the night he'd picked me up. Perhaps he'd be alone tonight too. It seemed too much to hope for, but now I'd considered it I had to call him, and if Iona answered I'd keep quiet and pretend it was a hoax call. I opened the heavy red door and felt in my trouser pockets for some change.

I dialled. It rang. I wondered how many rings I ought to allow before hanging up. Three? Four?

'Hello?' The voice sounded nervous. But at least it was Paul.

'It's Sarah. Can you talk?'

'Yes,' he said, and I could hear him relaxing, 'what's wrong?'

'Is Iona there?'
'No.'
'So you're alone?'
He laughed. 'Of course.'
'Can I come round?'
He paused. 'That would be nice.'
'I should be there in about ten minutes.'

I told him I wanted a shower. He nodded and returned to the lounge. Instead of sitting down, he picked up his drink and walked back to me. I stared at him, surprised and uncertain.

He smiled. 'It's okay, isn't it? I thought I'd come up for a chat.'

We walked upstairs. It was hard to imagine him pissing in this pink pastel room, let alone talking to me while I washed. He put down the toilet seat and sat down, chivalrously hiding his eyes. I looked at his feet as I undressed. New shoes. Too heavy for this fluffy carpet.

'What were you doing?' I asked.

'Drinking.' He chuckled. 'Watching TV.'

'Anything good?'

'Satellite. The Adult Channel.' He paused. 'It's not very adult.'

I wondered what he meant by this, uncertain if he was complaining because the programmes weren't explicit enough, or mocking the idea of pornography being an adult entertainment. I climbed into the shower.

'You can look now,' I said, hidden behind the screen.

He stayed with me throughout my shower, even though I found it hard to make out his words beneath the running water. When I turned off the shower he held out a towel for me, wrapping the material around my wet body. He offered me a second towel for my hair, but I told him I'd kept my head away from the water. He smiled proudly at me, as if I'd done this to please him. Ignoring my protests, he took me into his arms and carried me into his bedroom.

Paul carefully positioned me across the mattress, slowly unwrapping the towels and kissing the triangles of revealed skin. He pulled me softly down the bed so my legs could hang down and push up my pudenda as he lowered his lips. For a long time I'd been irritated by how proud Paul seemed when he sucked me, as if he was the only man in the world who still performed this unnatural and arcane act. But tonight I felt as if I could let him go on licking for ever, not stopping him until I reached my third tugging orgasm.

I stared at his face as he looked up at me, remembering the conspiratorial pleasure of our earliest lovemaking, when he'd never have dreamed of bringing me here. His contented expression reminded me how sleeping together had once seemed a natural extension of our working relationship, and I wondered when that ease had been lost.

He undressed and climbed in next to me, turning my body so my back was against him. He let his erection press against me, then pulled back and left me to imagine it, waiting. He played with the wisps of hair at the nape of my neck. The pressure of his fingers was replaced by soft kisses. He was whispering. I felt entranced as he murmured to himself, moving his fingers down to massage my shoulders. His cock again, a sudden push. Then his hands, coming round to scoop up my breasts. He held me, tight. I let him play with my nipples, then I thrust my bum against his cock. I wanted him, more than I had for months. I tried to move myself round onto him, trapping his cock between my legs. He pulled back, but I had him, and I could tell he wanted to enter me.

I rubbed his cock between my thighs, teasing him until he rose up and pushed me face down against the mattress. Sex always seems to come in only two varieties: soft and slow or hard and fast. Tonight he fucked me slow and hard, each thrust opening me right up and then giving me time to feel the slow melt as he pulled back. He kept this steady motion longer than he ever had before, pushing and pushing until it felt neither pleasurable nor painful, but nevertheless filled me with a maddening need for him not to stop. I knew he'd dried me out and I'd ache afterwards, but every time I felt him slow down, I thrust back and urged him on. It didn't stop until he slid out and started touching himself before I could get him back in. He turned me over and straddled my body, rubbing at his wet cock. He shifted his large bum up higher, setting himself against my breastbone and working his cock with his knuckles knocking against my chin. I heard him gasp just before his sperm shot up over my nose and lips.

I wrapped myself around Paul's body, wanting to hold him all night. He kissed me and tried to pull away.

'What's wrong?' I asked.

'Nothing. I've got something for you.'

'A present?'

'Yes, but it's downstairs, so if you could please let go of me.'

I released him. He left the room. I lay back and stared at the ceiling, wondering what he'd bought me. I heard the stairs creak as he came back up. He came through the doorway with a bottle of champagne and two glasses.

'Are we celebrating?'

'Yes. I've been saving this for you, but we've had so little time together I thought I'd have to drink it on my own.'

'What's the occasion?'

'The pier.'

'What's happened?'

'Put it this way. It's still not certain that I'll be able to get the club going, but if it does work out, this is the moment that it became more than just a fantasy. It's a green-lighted project.'

I smiled. In spite of everything, I still felt proud for Paul. And even though I'd ruined my dress on the beach, part of me still wanted to be standing in that spotlight.

He uncorked the champagne, hopping backwards as he braced the bottle against his chest. He poured out a glass and handed it to me.

'Where's Iona?' I asked.

'She's staying with a friend. We've decided to spend the occasional weekend apart. It's an experiment. Her idea.'

He filled his own glass and got into bed, leaving the bottle on the bedside table. I rubbed his back.

'I'm sorry, I didn't mean to upset you. I just wondered if I could stay the night.'

He looked at me. 'Yeah, that's fine.' He paused, looking at the clock. 'As long as you're off early. She sometimes pops back on Saturday mornings. Do you want to watch some TV?'

'Okay.'

He took the remote from the table and aimed it at the television. He changed station a few times before settling on a film. It wasn't the Adult Channel, but an action movie with two mismatched policemen. I watched for a while, mainly because I enjoyed being cuddled up against Paul's shoulder, then lay back against the pillows and fell asleep.

My dreams that night centred around Jim. I kept seeing his red tracksuit and rotten teeth, his very presence a bad omen. In one of the dreams he was a figure on a Tarot card, dealt out to me by an old student friend telling my fortune. In another segment, he was falling from a mountain, and I had an important task to complete before he hit the ground. In my last dream before waking, he was a contestant on *Blind Date*, answering questions with descriptions of the violent acts he'd perpetrated on young women. When I woke up, it was still early, and I had plenty of time to wonder why my most vivid dreams had occurred under this roof.

S

Saturday

There's no such thing as a sincere apology. No one ever really feels sorry, just worried about the state of their soul, or their relationship. If someone lets me down I'd much rather they disappeared than made me listen to their inevitably inadequate explanations. I can forgive anybody anything as long as I never have to see them again.

After Friday, I thought it'd be best to make Mary take me away for the weekend. A brief disappearance would rebalance things between Neil and me. I find it so much easier to be the one in the wrong. But I couldn't bring myself to admit my jealousy to Mary, and resigned myself to returning home. Waiting for Neil that morning, I wished he was dead. I knew no excuse would be good enough, and hated myself for caring.

I did at least have a moment to prepare myself. Hearing Neil flirting with Sylvia as he came up to my room, I caught my ridiculous surge of crossness and forced myself to swallow it back down.

'Hello Sarah,' he said, looking at me. I waited. Any shrug of the shoulders, any sheepish smile, any sign of any amusement at all, and it'd all be over. But he clearly cared enough to keep a straight face.

'I can explain,' he began, 'it'll sound pathetic but I can explain. I didn't want you to see me in the state I was in last night. I thought it was better for you to be angry with me when I could manage a coherent apology.'

'I waited for ages.'

'I tried to get someone to tell you, but they didn't understand what I was saying.' He sighed. 'I had to be carried home.'

'You don't sound too bad today.'

'I know.' He sat on the bed. 'It's always like that with me. As long as I get it out my system the night before, I'm fine the next day. I hardly had a hangover at all. Even managed a fried breakfast.'

I nodded, and told him, 'I'm going to see a friend this afternoon.'

'Okay. What time?'

'Three.'

He looked at his watch. 'That still gives us an hour. Let me make it up to you.'

I sat next to him, still angry but glad to be held. He kissed my ears, a good way to avoid looking at my face. I felt him kiss down the line of my jaw, then let him push me back onto my small bed. He was moving quickly, as if expecting me to stop him. His fingers reached up to my breasts, pushing beneath the wire of my cups and grasping my flesh. His urgency pleased me, and I felt happy to let endorphins make things okay. He unbuttoned my jeans and pulled down my knickers, tugging his own trousers open and pushing them down to his knees. I reached out to stroke him, but he moved my hand away. He got rid of his boxers and kicked the tangled material onto the floor. He grabbed my legs and yanked them up and open, tipping me backwards. He rose up to enter me, clutching my buttocks and pulling my cunt against him. His thighs banged against the wooden frame of my bed as he fucked me, the rocking mattress making the sex seem more violent than it actually was. He held my bum the whole time, getting close then slowing down, again and again until he finally came.

I didn't really have anyone to visit at three. I got rid of Neil anyway, knowing if he stayed too long my resentment would return. Making that excuse had made me believe I really was going to see someone, and I decided to call in on Amy. Vanessa might be more fun, but I wanted someone to calm me down.

Amy's father answered the door. I remembered getting drunk in his lounge and felt guilty and awkward. It had been ages since I'd met someone's father and knew he was probably wondering why an older woman was hanging around his daughter. It seemed odd that I felt closer in age to Amy's father than Amy when she was nineteen and he looked at least twenty years older than me.

'We work in the bowling alley together,' I said, hoping that mentioning Amy's job would make my presence acceptable.

'Oh,' he said, and I was relieved to see his expression change, 'well, I know you're not Vanessa, so you must be Sarah.'

I nodded. Amy's father looked friendly enough, and I remembered Amy telling me about her mother's death. I felt envious of these two and their time together, remembering how much I had enjoyed spending time with my dad.

'Amy's upstairs,' he said, 'if you want to go on up.'

He stepped back and let me into the house. I walked up the stairs past the copper engravings and decided the room where the music was playing was Amy's. I knocked on the door and she told me to come in. She was lying on her bed reading a copy of *Cosmopolitan*. Seeing her relaxing like that reminded me of being at home, and the freedom I'd once had not to have to do anything.

'I didn't leave it unlocked, did I?' she asked.

'What?'

'The Dolphin. I was so distracted on Thursday. Vanessa was having one of her fits. How terrible is it? Did someone break in? I understand if you've come here to fire me.'

'Relax, this is a social call.'

She stared at me, then looked away. 'Really? Would you like a drink of something?' She moved across on the bed, and called to her father.

'No, that's okay,' I said, feeling embarrassed.

'What's wrong, Amy?' her father shouted.

'Are you sure you don't want something?' Amy asked. I nodded, and she shouted down, 'Nothing, Dad, it's okay.' She got up. 'I'll turn the stereo down.'

Her bedroom was just like my sister's had been. The same faces on the posters; the same china sculptures and aromatherapy candles. The only difference was that apart from a yellow puppy, Amy's cuddly toys had been banished to the cupboard.

I wanted to hold Amy and stroke her hair, but I realised this would terrify her. So I said, 'What was Vanessa having a fit about?'

'Nothing, well, something, but it's a secret and I promised, so if I tell you, keep it to yourself, okay?'

I nodded.

'She's slept with another guy.'

'But I thought that was what she wanted to do.'

'It is.'

'So where's the problem? Was it horrible?'

'It's complicated. Okay, I shouldn't say this, but the guy she slept with was Adrian.'

I thought of my shift partner and then Vanessa, trying to imagine them together. I remembered Adrian telling me how frightening he found it to be home alone, and hoped he was smart enough to realise this was a one-off.

'Shit.'

'Exactly,' she said. 'Vanessa thought it was nice, but it was *Adrian*, so she didn't feel anything for him.'

'So why's she upset?'

'Lots of reasons. She's upset because having sex with Adrian made her remember how nice it was with Lee. She only slept with Adrian because she knew he'd be nice and easy to forget, but now she feels that her life's going to be this grand tragedy because she'll be sleeping with all these men she doesn't really like and all the time she'll be thinking of Lee.'

'Why doesn't she go back to him?'

'She can't now. She's humiliated him, and besides, Vanessa's got a romantic idea of how relationships should be. Breaking up with Lee and sleeping with someone else has ruined that relationship for her, and she'd hate to get involved with him again. It's too fucked up to make her happy.'

I looked at Amy, envious that Vanessa had her to confide in. Amy would never betray Vanessa the way Lesley had betrayed me. She was more like my sister, who cherished every detail I gave her and held my life in her mind with every possibility mapped out and remembered. I wanted to tell Amy about all my problems, starting with Charlie and Lesley, going through Paul, Henry and Neil, and ending up here.

'So what's she going to do?' I asked Amy.

'I don't know,' she replied. 'She was like this about a guy once before, but then Lee came along and pulled her out of it. So if she finds someone who's okay, everything should be fine. If she doesn't find someone, then I don't know.

Vanessa's the kind of woman who needs to be in a steady relationship.'

I swallowed. 'Amy,' I asked, 'would you like to go out with me tonight? We could go to The Princess like we did before.'

Amy looked at me. 'Tonight? I'm sorry, I'm going out for a meal with Ben. But why don't you ask Vanessa? She could probably do with talking to you.'

'Okay. Thanks, Amy, that's a good idea.'

I didn't bother calling on Vanessa. I was going to spend tonight alone with a bottle of vodka and a magazine. I bought the drink from the off-licence and a copy of *Company* from a newsagents. Then I walked back to Sylvia's.

I listened to the radio all afternoon, listlessly wandering down for the evening meal. After eating, I talked to Sylvia for a bit then went upstairs for a bath, hoping the hot water would help slow me down. I returned to my bedroom wrapped in a towel, flopping naked on the bed. I lay there for a few seconds, telling myself I ought to comb my hair to stop it getting tangled. Then I heard the loud bleep of my alarm clock. I reached across and hit the silence button but the sound continued, coming from beneath the mattress. I knelt on the floor and reached under the frame of the bed. My fingers immediately located a small square that felt like another clock. I pulled it out. Neil's pager. I pressed the buttons at the front, trying to stop the noise. The screen read:

10. HOW DID IT GO WITH SARAH?

I stared at the words, feeling nervous. There was nothing about the message that should trouble me. I knew it was from Mary, unless someone else knew about Neil's pager. (Maybe his parents? It wasn't impossible that he'd told them about me and this was how he kept in contact with them.) I knew they were friends, and that although she'd made me feel I was getting her exclusive attention, Mary was probably just as intimate with Neil as she was with me. And the message was only a friendly inquiry, the sort of thing she might ask in the office. But, nevertheless, I sensed it might be best to put the pager on my bedside table and forget about it. It seemed too obvious a record of an unknown world.

I uncapped my Smirnoff and poured myself a glass, still holding the pager in my left hand. I thought of Paul, kneeling beside his wife's bedside drawer, and how scathing I'd felt about his desire to know his lover's secrets. Then I pressed the black message back button:

09. GOOD BOY. YOU WON'T REGRET IT.

I told myself that Paul also left Neil messages, and this second line still didn't mean anything. I pressed again:

08. MAKE SOMETHING UP.

And again:

07. SO WILL PAUL.

I sipped from my glass, and, unable to stop myself, pressed the button a further six times:

06. I'M SUPPOSED 2 SEE PAUL.

05. SEE ME INSTEAD.

04. BEING JIM. WHAT R U DOING TONIGHT?

03. FREAK SARAH OUT.

02. TERRIBLE, THANKS TO JIM.

01. ARE YOU COMING IN TOMORROW?

Reading that final message, I pictured Mary lying across

Paul's bed. Her legs were open. One foot lay in Neil's lap, the other in Paul's. The two men exchanged smiles, and peeled the childrens' plasters from her blistered heels. I wondered if it was paranoid to imagine she'd been to bed with both of them at the same time. Clearly, I wasn't paranoid enough. Not guessing Neil and Mary had slept together was naïve, but I'd been so certain Paul had given up on her.

Okay, so I had to take this seriously. What had I learnt? It was important to treat the pager as an anonymous source of information. Messages 1–4 clearly referred to my night out with Mary and my reaction to running into Jim. Message 10 was inconclusive, but seemed to be about Neil's visit this morning. But messages 5–9 were the important ones, seeming to suggest that Mary was having affairs with both Neil and Paul, and that last night Paul had been expecting Mary. The pager also indicated that while Paul and I were together, so were Neil and Mary. It didn't seem unrealistic to assume that all the messages were from Mary to Neil.

All I could think of was how I prided myself on never trusting anyone. It was ludicrous that this had happened to me. I wasn't squeamish, and confronted myself with unpalatable truths all the time. I thought about all the lies the trio had told me (that was the only way I could see them now, as a *trio*), and looked for any discrepancy I should've noticed. I was happy to hate myself for refusing to believe that I could be betrayed, but everything fitted, right back to Mary's arrival.

I climbed into bed, clutching my bottle of vodka and trying to stop my brain working back through the last few weeks. I remembered Mary sobbing as she told me she slept with me because she was scared of going to bed with men, and realised at that time she must've been fucking both Paul and Neil. That kind of deceit went beyond the track-covering of infidelity. Those kind of lies were pathological. I dropped my glass. It smashed. Fuck it. I swigged straight from the bottle, praying the drink would paralyse my mind before my anger could prompt me to action.

Shortly before I passed out, I found myself feeling grateful to Neil's pager, as if it was a friend who'd passed on secrets it thought I ought to know. It seemed less demeaning to find out about these betrayals from a machine, sparing me of the horror of Paul or Neil or Mary (or, worse still, the three of them together) sitting down and telling me what they'd been up to. I thought of Charlie and how he'd described his love for Lesley as if telling a story he expected me to admire. I wondered if situations like this had ever been imagined when they invented the pager, and fell asleep imagining a future where every love affair was controlled by technology, picturing white-coated strangers monitoring betrayals on computer screens, eyebrows raised in endless amazement.

5

Sunday

Three taps was all it took to bring me back. In spite of all the precautions I'd taken to ensure I got through Sunday morning without a conscious thought, Henry's gentle rap on my bedroom door instantly snapped me back into the world, and I awoke terrified I'd forgotten something.

'It's only me, Sarah. I thought you might like to come to church with me.'

I wondered why Sylvia had let him come up. She was supposed to protect me from unexpected visits. I wasn't in a fit state to see anyone, but I didn't want my last memory of Henry to be his voice on the other side of a door.

'Okay,' I said, 'I'll meet you there.'

'Right,' he replied. 'We'll be sitting at the back.'

I grasped my forehead, wondering who he was with. After last night, I expected him to have come here with Paul and Neil, the three of them returning to tell me about their homosexual *ménage à trois. At least you've still got your sense of humour,* I told myself, the voice in my head an echo of my mother's. My puritan side thought a morning in church might be just what I needed, and

I stepped over the broken glass by my bed to find some clothes.

I arrived just after the service had started. I recognised Anne-Marie before I noticed Henry beside her. Anne-Marie was wearing a purple jumper with black vinyl stripes sewn into the material over an electric orange skirt. It seemed odd that such cheap, ugly clothes would make someone look that carnal, and I felt ashamed at my disgust for her. Henry wore a white shirt buttoned to the collar with no tie, and a pair of fawn trousers. They were sitting at the back of the church, in the same pew where Henry had touched me up a few weeks before.

I sat next to Anne-Marie, taking a hymn book from the shelf in front of us. The vicar was quoting a passage from John's gospel which depicted Jesus walking on water. He seemed younger than I remembered him, and became more animated as he moved on to tell the congregation how he thought there was something magical about living in a seaside town that prompted frequent contemplation of God. He spoke about how other people had suggested that Weston was an irreligious place, and how ridiculous he found this. His words temporarily removed *the trio* from my thoughts, and I remembered Henry telling me about Miss Weston. At the end of the service, Henry touched my hand and asked if I'd come to The Wayfarer with them.

I could tell it was serious because Henry wasn't eating. It came as little surprise that Anne-Marie refused food, but I was amazed Henry was skipping Sunday lunch. I'd suffered too much recent trauma to miss my meal, and if this pair were about to upset me again, I thought I might at least get a good feed out of it.

'First things first,' said Henry, stretching his arm across the table, 'have you come to a decision about my offer?'

I looked down at the table, wondering why I'd thought so little about this. Money rarely troubled me, even when I was down to my last few pounds, but in my head I could hear my father and Paul urging me not to be stupid.

'I'm sorry,' I told him, 'I can't accept.'

'Ah,' he said, 'that's a shame. That makes things more difficult.'

I waited. Anne-Marie put her hand over her father's, encouraging him.

'There's no easy way of telling you this. Anne-Marie and I are going on a cruise.'

Anne-Marie smiled at me as the waitress put my plate on the table. I looked at the happy pride in her eyes and wondered if there'd ever been a time when Henry had considered taking me on this cruise. Maybe it was only in retrospect that I noticed this, but I was sure there had been moments last Thursday afternoon when Henry was looking at me and considering the strength of our attachment. Perhaps he thought I'd turn him down. Before last night, I would've done.

'Are you sure you won't take the money?' he asked. 'I won't be around for a long time. I know things are okay for you now, but I wouldn't like to think of you being in trouble and wishing you'd accepted my offer.'

I touched his hand. Anne-Marie winced. 'I'm very grateful, Henry, but money's the least of my problems.'

He nodded, and looked at his daughter. 'Okay. Excuse our rudeness, but I think it's probably best if we leave you to your dinner. I know how hard it is to eat with someone else watching you.'

He stood up, and let Anne-Marie out. The two of them walked across the tiled floor to the exit, and Henry held the door open for his daughter. I watched them walk past my window. Henry stopped, said something to Anne-Marie, and came back.

'I didn't want her to see this,' he said, turning his back to Anne-Marie and taking an envelope from his pocket. 'I'm going to leave this on the table. You can't stop me doing that.'

He kissed me on the forehead. I watched him walk away. As he rejoined his daughter, I said quietly: 'Enjoy your cruise.'

The envelope, inevitably, was packed with twenty-pound notes. The sum scared me, and I felt eager to start getting rid of it. Few shops would be open on a Sunday, but I wasn't that worried about what I spent the money on. I cut through to a street of gift shops and chemists, feeling reckless and sad.

Back at Sylvia's, I examined my hoard.

I'd begun with magazines, buying women's monthlies, pop glossies, pornography: anything with a woman on the cover. Then I'd bought a sun visor, a plastic hat, a red bikini, a packet of cigarettes, and a bucket and spade. In the chemist, I'd bought make-up, blue hair dye, and paid an old lady ten pounds for her prescription pills. I wasn't going to take them (I didn't even know if they'd do any damage) but in my melodramatic mood they seemed a good purchase.

I also bought a pair of hairdressing scissors. When I bought them I had no intention of cutting my hair, but looking at the glinting handles lying on my bed, the idea seemed less foolish than it had in the shop. In the chemists, I'd been feeling crazy, impulsive, but still reigned in by common sense. Cutting my hair seemed something I might contemplate but never actually do. Now, though, I wasn't sure. After all, there was no reason why a trim should do me any harm.

I broke the spine on my copy of *Escort*, and spread the glossy pages beneath the legs of my chair. I'd never bought pornography before, and now my impulsiveness had passed, I felt surprised by my daring. I wished I'd noticed the look on the newsagent's face when my pile of magazines was rung up, but I couldn't even remember if I'd been served by a man or a woman.

It felt strange to have all these naked women smiling up at me, and I laughed at my behaviour. But I knew I had to give myself a release, and this seemed the most harmless way of getting rid of my anger. Still, I worried about the speed with which I was doing things, and once I'd spread out the magazines, I sat down and took five deep breaths. It was no use cutting my hair with shaking hands, and I could afford a minute to calm down.

The telephone rang. I trembled as I picked it up.

'Yes?'

'Sarah? It's Charlie.'

I knew. I remembered his voice immediately, even though I hadn't heard it in over a year. I felt terrified, especially when I heard him breathing into the receiver. I couldn't believe Lesley had been brave enough to give him my number.

'Is this a private call?'

'What d'you mean?'

'Is Lesley there? Is Mum there? Are they all sitting round you?'

'They don't know I'm calling.'

He waited. I believed him.

'So what do you want?'

'Lesley said things are going well for you.'

'They were.'

I heard him exhale. The phone crackled and I imagined him settling back. 'It feels strange, doesn't it? Talking again.'

I lay back on the mattress. 'It was weird to see Lesley.'

'I told her not to go. I knew you wouldn't want to see her.'

'What about living with my mum? Doesn't that feel odd to you?'

'You weren't here, Sarah. You don't know how bad things got.'

I paused, then said, 'So, go on then, tell me about Melissa.'

'What?'

'That must be next. What's she done now, hung herself with a pair of my old tights?'

'Perhaps I shouldn't have called.'

I pulled my duvet around me, pressing my ear against the receiver to find some clue as to where he was. I couldn't hear any street sounds, and I wondered if he'd had to wait until Mum and Lesley went out before making the call. I wondered if he felt guilty about phoning me. I knew he wouldn't hang up first, but I didn't know whether he was willing to talk about us. I took a risk and said: 'Lesley said you dream about me.'

He sighed. 'Of course I do.'

'I dream about you too.'

'Why don't you come home?' he asked.

'What would happen if I did?'

'We'd work it out.'

'My life there is over.'

'I miss you, Sarah.'

I listened to him breathe and thought about how often I dreamt about Charlie, even now. I remembered a summer afternoon when we drove to Hampton Court in my black Mini and I made a daisy chain for him half seriously and half as a joke and he accepted it solemnly, ceremoniously placing it around his neck as if it was the most important gift he'd ever been given. I remembered how safe I used to feel in his bed and how I never worried about having sex with him. I remembered how I never felt sore, never tensed, never worried he was thinking about someone else. And I remembered how much I'd wanted him to love me and how happy I was when he said he did.

Then I hung up.

I walked back to the mirror and started combing the knots out of my hair, cursing myself for letting it dry in the bed last night. Rediscovering my fringe was a painful process, and I had to dig my nails into my hands to distract myself from the burning in my scalp.

I held a small section of hair between two fingers and started snipping away. It was hard to get the length right, and even with a mirror positioned behind me, I couldn't really see the back. I cut off a centimetre at a time, thinking it best to start slowly. But it wasn't making any difference to my appearance so I held up a handful, wondering how I'd look with a bob. It was a risk but I wanted to do it, so I closed my eyes and closed the scissors through a year's worth of hair.

I couldn't be certain, but I thought it looked okay. The success of my venture made me look back at the blue hair dye, wondering if it was worth making one more experiment. It sounds extreme, but it wasn't permanent and easy to wash out. I looked at myself in the mirror, and ripped the lid from the packet.

I lay in bed in my new red bikini, blue hair staining the white pillows. I'd found Mary's Minnie Mouse sunglasses in my bedside drawer, and they proved the perfect conclusion to my outfit. I ran my fingers along my thighs and contemplated going round to see Paul and Mary. Paul had said Iona was coming back on Sunday afternoon, and in spite of my anger, I still felt a sense of loyalty to my boss. I didn't want to upset his wife unnecessarily, and it was important to me to resolve this with my dignity intact. I could visit Mary, but then she'd tell Paul, and I wanted to talk to him before he'd prepared his story. I had little choice but to wait until tomorrow. Frustrated by this delay, I pulled down my suitcase from the top of the wardrobe.

As I packed, I remembered how proud Henry had been about his ability to leave his room at any time. I remembered talking to him outside the church and pictured him and Anne-Marie returning to his room and her sitting on his bed and watching him comb his hair as I'd watched him in the past. I imagined him standing by the bin and throwing away his thrillers one by one, staring at the covers and trying to remember the plot of each but being unable to come up with any specific details.

I threw away my torn magazines and used toothpaste tubes and the cardboard box of my hair-dyeing kit. I opened my suitcase on the bed and filled it with my clothes. The only thing I left behind was the ruined PVC dress and Henry's envelope of cash to say thank you to Sylvia. The old lady's bottle of pills lay on the carpet. I picked it up, wondering what I'd paid ten pounds for. Sleeping tablets. Good. I took four, not enough to kill me but certain to get me through to Monday.

Monday

I turned away from Mary's door, needing to know exactly what I was going to say before knocking. I had to be prepared for her to be naked, in her nightclothes, in bed with Paul. Nothing could throw me, because if it did I'd lose control and say things I didn't mean and it'd take for ever to finish this.

I breathed out, then knocked. No response. I tried again. I heard movements, then she opened the door. I wondered why she'd put the chain on. Had she expected me? And if so, why was she scared? What did she expect me to do?

'Can I come in?'

She looked away. Was Paul in there? 'If you like. It's not very tidy.'

'I don't care.'

Mary pushed the door forward, slid off the chain and let me in. She was wearing a green towelling bathrobe. I looked at her shoulders, hearing a hysterical, self-pitying voice inside my head saying *But she's fatter than me*. I tried to remember the last time I'd looked her in the face, but all I could recall was her hands squeezing my shoulders. She was staring at me and I thought I saw guilt in her expression, but then I realised it was shock at the colour of my hair.

'Like it?' I asked, holding up a few strands. 'I think a woman has to keep changing if she expects to keep her man.'

I could tell this wasn't what she was expecting, and I wondered how she'd predicted my response. I imagined her and Paul lying in bed, laughing at me. Then I thought of her telling Neil about this later – *she turned up at the crack of dawn, and her hair was bright blue* – and him wondering what he'd seen in me.

'What's wrong?' she asked.

I'd brought along the pager to avoid talking about how I knew. I pressed it into her hand, saying: 'I suppose I ought to have paged you myself, really. Then we could've resolved this without speaking.'

Mary went to her handbag, pulling out a box of cigarettes. She offered one to me then started laughing, an angry, emotional sound that soon turned into tears. She rubbed at her eyes with the heel of her hand.

'I guess we're not friends any more.'

She hadn't been lying about her room being untidy. Everything packed away on the night of the dinner party was now spread across the floor. CDs sat in cigarette-paper nests. Trays of dirty plates lay alongside the settee. A black nylon body had almost made it to the bedroom, abandoned next to a twisted pair of knickers, a stuck-on sanitary towel visible inside the white material.

I sighed. 'I can take betrayal. What I can't understand is why you went to so much trouble to befriend me. I hardly spoke to any of the recruits before you. It would've been easy to seduce Paul without spending time with me.'

She pulled her bathrobe around her legs. 'I like you, Sarah. I meant all the stuff I said to you about being impressed by your intelligence. I've never met another woman like you. But that didn't stop me being attracted to Neil and Paul.'

'I don't even have female friends,' I said, still unable to understand how this situation had arisen.

She was really sobbing now. 'I'm sorry, Sarah. I'm so sorry.'

'No, no, don't be. You're the new model, that much is obvious. I'm just sorry I wasn't more graceful about giving up my crown.'

I left.

I knew the minute I got into work that Mary had tipped Paul off. He closed the door behind me and picked up a pen to fiddle with.

'We can still be honest, can't we, Paul?'

He stared at my hair. 'Of course.'

'Mary's spoken to you.'

'She said you were upset.'

'Only because you didn't tell me,' I said, using my friendliest, most adult tone. 'I was surprised.'

'There were a lot of things you didn't tell me either. I thought we were taking these relationships for granted. I had Iona, so you got Henry. You had Neil, so I got Mary.'

He stared at me. I felt more respect for Paul than I ever had for Neil and Henry, and I still wanted him to like me. I knew he was offering me as much as he could, and wanted to believe he was doing this because he realised I didn't need to be here. Then resentment returned: 'Just tell me one thing. Did you tell Mary about the pier?'

He paused. 'No.' I stared at him. He looked away. 'No, that's ours, and it always will be.'

I walked towards him, moving behind the desk and embracing him. 'I really loved you,' I told him, pressing my face into his hair.

He laughed. 'I love you too.'

Neil tried to talk to me on the way out. I mumbled a few words and pushed past him. He didn't try to stop me. I don't suppose I really expected him to. I ran down the stairs and past the solarium. I knew the women there would've loved a drama like this. An idiot like me could've kept them in conversation for weeks.

I don't know if Paul lied to me about the pier. It's hard to believe that he hadn't mentioned it to Mary, especially after he'd seen what an aphrodisiac effect it'd had on me. But I told myself it was silly to be upset by the smallest of his betrayals. And besides, Paul was right. I could hardly accuse him of cheating when I'd been out there ruining his dress on the Weston sands.

It was hot outside, and I wondered if I should get a taxi instead of sweating my way to the station. But I thought that as I'd never return to Weston, it was worth walking through it one last time. I walked quickly, swinging my suitcase from one leg to another and avoiding any locations that might make me think twice about my departure.

When I reached the station, I bought a ticket and a hot bacon sandwich. There was half an hour before my train was due, so I sat in the waiting room and listened to the muzak. I didn't recognise the song but it sounded beautiful, the weird arrangement and lack of words changing an old hit into a strange, disembodied melody that provided the perfect accompaniment to my departure from Weston.

Sunday

30th July

Dear Mum,

I don't intend to post this letter so if you've received it you'll know that something inside me has changed and I'm ready to tell the truth. I don't intend to post this letter, but I can't write it unless I imagine you reading it. This probably sounds confusing, but what I mean is that I have stuff to tell you that I can never imagine saying to your face, but maybe if I put it in a letter, it will resolve things and allow me to act in a sensible way with you.

I have your letters in front of me because I want to feel that this isn't one-sided and that I'm corresponding with you. I'm scared that I'll lose sight of the way you are now and rant on as if I'm some teenage girl railing against her parents. Maybe that's what you want me to do. You've mentioned several times in your letters that I seem too controlled, but that's the only way I can act honestly.

If you do ever get this letter there will be a postmark on it, but I promise you that postmark will bear no relation to where I'm living. I learnt lots of lessons from being in Weston, but the most important is that I will never allow myself to become tied to one place again. So if I post this, it will be as I'm leaving somewhere, because the last thing I want is for you to send Lesley after me again.

You said that the fact that I gave you my Weston address made you believe that I wanted you to write to me. That wasn't true. I know you'll think I'm only saying this to hurt you (you'll probably think that about a lot of things in this letter), but I really am just trying to be honest with you. I gave you my address so you wouldn't have to worry about me. I was going to send you a photograph of me by the beach so that whenever you worried about me you could look at my picture and know I was happy. But I knew you'd want to feel an ongoing connection so I gave you my address as an act of trust. You betrayed that trust, so I shall not make that mistake again.

I don't want this letter to sound like a whinge, and my knowledge that I wouldn't be able to put pen to paper without unleashing pages of resentment is what's stopped me writing before now, but I cannot write the truth if I do not go through the pain on the way. You asked what there was in Weston. There was nothing in Weston. That's why I was there.

If you see Dad again, please tell him I love him and miss him. You may find this hard to believe but I love you and miss you too. That doesn't mean I want to see either of you. I'm glad the two of you are speaking again. I always thought it was good that you didn't fight when you broke up, because it's the words spoken then that are hardest to forget. If you can't remember why you are angry with someone, there's no reason for you not to become friends again. But if you'll allow me to give you some advice (and please don't read anything into this), be gentle with Dad. He finds change difficult, and he has to be given time to adjust.

I felt sad that you think I've abandoned my father and sister. I ask of them only what I ask of you: some time to myself. I'm twenty-seven years old and I don't know who I am. I cannot communicate to you how terrifying that feels. I also feel sad that the way we behaved during the year Dad put his back out made you feel like an outsider. Anything we did together was designed to impress you, and rather than being private jokes, our fooling around was an act to make you love us.

I don't feel angry about you going through my room, and if you feel any guilt, rest assured I forgive you. I know how it feels to want to know someone's secrets, and my only regret is that I made you feel that frustrated. The reason why you found only dates and facts is because I took all my diaries and notebooks with me. I don't know why, because I would never read them, and I can't imagine showing them to someone else.

I don't know what to say about Charlie and Lesley. I'm angry at you for giving Lesley my address, and although I've told myself not to attack you for something I don't understand, I cannot help feeling upset that they are now living with you. Whatever any of you say, it is not normal for someone's mother to invite her daughter's ex-boyfriend and his new girlfriend to live with her. I want so much to admire you, but behaviour like that not only seems like a terrible weakness, but also a betrayal of my trust.

Every time I find myself getting wound up about this, I tell myself I'm being unfair and I try to picture how it might work out happily. I try to imagine you all gathered around a table – you, Dad, Charlie, Lesley, Melissa and her boyfriend – but it seems tragic and reminds me of the way families become when they have shared some public trauma. That's the real point, Mum, that's what I'm trying to say: you act as if you've all been united by cancer or a plane crash, and then tell me the real link is that you all love me. How do you think that makes me feel?

I know you hate me judging my sister, but please keep an eye on Melissa. I don't feel guilty about leaving her, but I would worry if your concern about me drew your attention away from her. Although you say you don't understand me, I think you and I have everything in common. But Melissa is like Dad, and if there is any danger in our family I think it lies with her. You seemed happy about her new boyfriend, and I'm not saying there's any reason why you shouldn't be, but when I heard what he was like, I felt scared. Melissa is different to me in that she has always sought out comfort. You probably don't think there's anything wrong with that, but it means that if anything does go wrong with her situation, she has no release left. So please try to get her to do something that is not connected to her boyfriend.

In your letter it seemed as if you thought I had no happy memories of my childhood. Don't you remember how lovely it was when Melissa and I were kids? I've always put my optimism down to the fact that before I experienced school and university, I was part of a united family that didn't need anyone else. All my friends' mothers always seemed so weary, so resentful of their children. I loved the way you made me feel my company and the things I said to you were valuable. It shouldn't surprise you that the thing that started all this was going to Weston with you and Melissa. I always think of those trips when I wonder why I feel closer to you and Melissa than I do to Dad. You found somewhere that made us all happy and allowed us to revel in it. You taught us how to seek pleasure without feeling guilty. Most of those trips blur into one in my memory, but the last time remains separate from the rest.

Maybe it was because we knew it was the last time, but on that trip everything was right. All those other trips were nice, but there was always something that went wrong, as if fate had to stop us from achieving perfect happiness. The saddest example was the time when Melissa lost her Mickey Mouse balloon. But, anyway, this day was perfect. We went in the bowling alley, the arcades, had a nice lunch in The Wayfarer. You got to walk across the beach and collect shells. We had candy floss and a donkey ride. Then, just as we were about to go, Melissa noticed one of those boards where there's holes for faces and you get a picture of yourself looking like someone else. There were three holes, a vicar, a mermaid, and a strongman. It was stupid but Melissa begged you to let us get our picture taken. It cost a pound and you only had ten pence left. Anyone else would have refused, but you knew – I know you knew – that this would be the disappointment that would mar this perfect day. So you went to an arcade and you gambled the last ten pence (knowing you were risking an even bigger disappointment) and you won. I wish I had a copy of that photograph, and I'll always remember that special day.

Love,
Sarah